THE SONS OF NOAH
OF NOAH
& OTHER STORIES

THE SONS OF NOAH
& *OTHER STORIES*

JACK CADY

Broken Moon Press □ Seattle

These stories first appeared, in earlier forms, in the following publications: "Sons Of Noah" was first published in *OMNI*, January 1991 (copyright © 1991 by OMNI Publications International Ltd.); "Now We Are Fifty" in *Tattoo* (Circinatum Press, 1978); "Resurrection" and "The Patriarch" in *The Chariton Review* (1978, 1986); "Tinker" in *Glimmer Train* (1992); "The Curious Candy Store" in *Pulphouse* (1990); and "By Reason Of Darkness" in *Prime Evil* (New American Library, 1988). Reprinted here by permission.

Printed in the United States of America.

ISBN 0-913089-40-0
Library of Congress Catalog Card Number 92-72433

Cover image © 1992 by Nick Gregoric. Used by permission of the artist.

Project editor: Lesley Link
Proofreaders: Ken Sánchez and Audrey Thompson

Broken Moon Press
Post Office Box 24585
Seattle, Washington 98124-0585 USA

For William Pitt Root

Contents

THE SONS OF NOAH

□   □   □

THE SONS OF NOAH

And the fear of you and the dread of you shall be
upon every beast of the earth, and upon all fowl
of the air, upon all that moveth *upon* the earth,
and upon all the fishes of the sea; into your hand
are they delivered. —*Genesis 9:2*

WHEN DARKNESS EDGES THROUGH THIS VALLEY, SHAD-
ing slow figures of cattle moving toward milking barns, last light
falls on the weathered steeple of Sons Of Noah Church. The
church stands on stilts beside Troublesome Creek, as do all our
barns and houses. The valley is a flood plain.

Visitors to our Northwest valley always ask why we, the
country people, stay in a place bound to flood every seven years.
Why do we choose to live in houses foundationed on twenty-foot
timbers hewn from ancient cedars. Why live where cattle climb
ramps to elevated barns. We reply that floods renew the soil and
make good pasture. Our milk and produce are the purest in the
world. What we say is not false.

What we do not say is that this valley casts a spell. It is shadowed by eight-thousand-foot mountains. The valley is twenty
miles long, seventeen miles wide. Weather systems bred in the
Aleutians bring rain nine months each year. Darkness often covers
the land, even in daylight, and not all darkness is threatening. The
mountains are protectors, because the world beyond these mountains is beset by demons.

From this mountain valley our sons sometimes go away to
the Army. Those who survive always return, and they tell crazy
tales. They speak of endless streams of automobiles, and of demonic voices chattering from television screens. They speak of
billboards and politicians, wars, suicides, whoring, rape, drugs,
satanic worship.

Visitors describe us as 'peculiar', and maybe that is true. On
the other hand, we hear of the outside world and describe it as in-

sane. We do not mind if the rest of the world chooses insanity, as long as that world leaves us alone. At least, we have not minded until now.

I am elected to write of this. My name is Thaddeus Morris, which of course means little, although around here the name carries weight. I am not the oldest man in the valley—the oldest is our preacher, Jubal Petersen—but I'm old enough. My fingers are crabbed around the pen as I write, and lamplight, fueled by finely rendered sheep fat, glows smoky and slick across these pages which aim at your salvation. We do not want to harm you. We wish to be known as builders, not destroyers. We hope you will be warned.

Allow me to show how life is with us, then tell the sad story of a terrible destruction which has caused us to become troubled. I must recount a bit of history.

Our ancestors came to this Pacific Northwest from upper New York State in the 1860s, following the Oregon Trail. They had strong leadership and holy purpose. From their very beginnings they called themselves The Sons Of Noah. Their beliefs centered around the mistakes and sins of Noah after The Flood. They saw themselves as quiet people who would eventually reclaim the world through decent behavior and piety. Old diaries kept by womenfolk tell of that harsh trek, of worn-out Conestogas, of privation, of dying oxen, of Indian raiders.

Our people found coastal Oregon over-populated. Trees fell before pioneer ambitions. Log houses sometimes stood no more than a thousand rods apart. Indians wearing seal skins, or colorfully dyed cedar bark robes, clustered around settlements. They traded furs for guns and whiskey. The world seemed filled with bustle.

The leader in those days was a man named Aaron Schmidt. In prayers Schmidt received solace, and in dreams he received direction. There was a Northwest valley, he was told, avoided even by the Indians. In written records the harsh journey northward to the Olympic Peninsula is known as 'The Pilgrimage'.

This valley finally lay revealed. It lies two thousand feet

above sea level, and above a mighty rainforest. Our pastures are vibrant and lush, and the darkness of this valley is a good thing. With more sun the pastures' growth would carry frenzy.

A road now runs part way in, but the last two miles are corduroy road, suited only to ox carts. These days we sell produce and cheese to merchants who monthly send trucks to the head of the road.

That original congregation arrived, and first built a church and a graveyard. The long pilgrimage took its toll on older members, including Schmidt. The earliest grave markers were simple stones from the mountainside. To this day they sit as squat reminders of faith among the multitude of carved markers. In a hundred years many are born, and many die.

The original congregation looked about in wonder. Grass grew lush, and a constant supply of pure water ran in Troublesome Creek. The valley spawned life. Our forefathers took two-hundred-pound fish from the creek, fish so bizarre that they seemed ancient as creation. Fish with teeth like the canines of wolves. Fish with winglike fins—that when tanned became fine leather—and walking fish with appendages stiff as legs. Bear and cougar and elk shuffled and stalked and ran through the valley. Beaver and possum, weasels, foxes and wolverine contested for food and life. Our people gave thanks in prayer, but they were also mystified.

These days we have more knowledge, because we are not averse to new ideas. We learn a great deal, because we take in more of the world's coin than we can possibly spend. Our only purchases from that outside world are salt and books. We study books of today and books of the past. In this way we figure out our world.

Our valley sits atop a great fissure. When these mountains were created, the rock structure split, then tumbled back on itself. Beneath our feet lies a primeval lake. Troublesome Creek, which seldom runs more than forty feet wide, is also bottomless. Living water from melting snow in the mountains runs along the surface of the creek. It passes over water that may be two thousand feet deep, or more. The rock is impermeable. The entire fissure holds water as old as the original creation. We do not know everything that lives down there, but sometimes we get indications. It works this way.

Every seventh year the valley floods. There are Biblical explanations for this, but none are scientific. As flood spreads across our fields we check our boats. Water does not often rise more than ten or twelve feet, while our houses are twenty feet above ground. Only twice in this century has water risen to cover the floors of our houses. In 1917 it rose to twenty-one feet. In 1942 it rose to twenty-three. Flood covers the graveyard like a protecting hand, and no grave is ever disturbed. Even the upright markers do not tilt.

For those years of highest water we have flatboats to carry our horses, oxen, cattle, sheep, fowl, and swine. Ordinarily we pass between houses and barns and church in rowboats. Water rises quickly. Flood replenishes the land, and the flood seems driven by a mind of its own. Waters flow, then concentrate. Some years they may greatly enrich the Jensen acres, sometimes the Petersen's, or other farms. The valley lies for forty days beneath flood, then water slides away, down the mountains or into the fissure of Troublesome Creek.

The water level sometimes drops quickly. Huge shapes flee across fields, dashing back to the safety of deep water. Silver streaks intermix. They are flashes of light sparkling above the drowned pasture. When water drops too quickly, strange fish are stranded in the fields, although there is a type of fish that is never stranded. The variety is fleet and many-colored, like shooting rainbows through the torrent. These fish have nearly human eyes, but larger, seeing wider than do we. It is a busy time for our whole community.

Men harness horses and oxen to huge mud sleds. The sleds skid to the fields, and a process of selection begins. We try to protect the original creation. Those fishes still living get dumped back in the creek. Then the men use pitchforks to load the rest onto the sleds. There is no waste of the creation. Men dress out the fish, and women dry them. We have never had seven lean years here, but are prepared should they occur. Twice there have been fish that had to be towed by two oxen.

And so we live, living among the primal forces and original fury that brought this planet into being. Power grows. We walk beside great waters.

On Sundays, after services, we gather in front of Sons Of Noah Church: the Andersens, the Jensens, Adams, Schmidts, and two dozen other families. Traditionally, it is a time of quiet joy.

Beside the church, the churchyard with its gravestones becomes a living presence. Our ancestors lie at our very elbows, so to speak. Children, who have learned to sit patiently through morning services, romp among the graves. They are like flitting butterflies, brightly colored, dancing in games of hide-and-seek behind tombstones.

We talk among ourselves, the way our people have sought truth since the 1860s. We used to discuss crops and ideas. Unhappy I am to report that these days we are forced to speak of power.

A demonic world presses close. Aircraft sometimes pass overhead, where once passed only the birds of the air. More beasts of the field, deer and elk and wolves, are driven to our high valley as a demonic world logs the rainforest. We are careful in our speech.

"We do not command these waters. To think we command is the sin of pride." Our preacher, Jubal Petersen, says this. He was once a man of immense strength, and even in his age he still drives oxen. His shoulders are square, and his hair is a cloud of white above a high and furrowed brow.

The children play. Here and there young wives and husbands whisper together. One girl's waist has grown. In a few months there will be birth and christening. The generations are intact.

Men stand in silence, waiting for the spirit of truth to guide their words. We are not a hasty people. The men are fair of face. Their suits are subdued colors of gray, blue, brown. Work-hardened hands hang restful at their sides. The men stand like protecting trees of the mountain forests.

"Do we serve at the threshold of divine power?" one says. His name is Lars Landstrup, his father was Eric, his grandfather was Sven. Lars' strength is great, and, of all of us, he worries most about right and wrong. "Maybe," he says, "we protect the creation."

"The waters protect us," a woman murmurs. Mercy Adams is a grandmother now, but there is that about her which recalls the beauty of her youth. If our women have a leader, then surely Mercy leads. "We are in delicate balance," she says. She glances toward the younger women, toward the young wife who is with child.

The graveyard lies silent, except for children's play. Our women stand like flowers. They dress in gowns showing the many colors of natural dyes. Above the graveyard the steeple rises like a benediction.

"Our cause is just," another woman murmurs.

"We do none of this for gain," a man says. "We are not engaged in spurious adventures."

Our disputations rise because some men from that outside world are most hideously dead. We fear that we had a hand in matters. We do not yet question the tenets of our faith, but clearly something is askew. Our ancestors believed that their quiet ways and piety would overcome the world. They believed in the power of reverence, not the power of force.

And yet great forces aid us. Power accumulates. I must now record the manner of those terrible deaths.

□   □   □

We did not immediately understand that the man was insane. Perhaps we might have helped him. One cannot hate the insane, only pity them. At the same time, if a wolverine gets loose in your streets it must be contained.

On an April morning last year, when sun glowed like a blessed spirit through mountain mist, the solitary figure of a man appeared at the head of the road. His outfit exceeded his need. Perhaps such waste should have warned us. He wore wool knickers, tall boots with much lacing, and a down parka quilted like a sleeping bag. His rolled pack rode on heavy shoulders, a pack filled with enough implements and supplies to last—if he knew what he was doing—for many months in the forest wilderness. Yet he had only hiked in two miles from the paved road where he left his truck.

And the truck, itself, was another mark of insanity, had we been clever enough to read its meaning. One of our sons who has been outside described it as an all-terrain vehicle. The truck proved capable of driving over rough country but was too small to haul anything. We thought it rather silly.

We have always welcomed our few visitors to this valley. We've hoped they would feel the serenity of this place, thus learn to be serene. Our message of piety would go with them when they returned to the outside world.

The man was bluff, but friendly. At the same time, he at first spoke to us as if we were children. He was a man accustomed to commanding others. In the grand illusion of his power he regarded us as simple, ignorant folk. We have had other visitors who thought us simpleminded. We always tolerate their pride, knowing they will leave.

For three days he camped at the head of the valley. The Jensen family invited him to supper and offered him a bed in the large room used by their sons. The man Hamilton, "Joe Hamilton to my friends," he said, took supper but refused the bed. He pitched his tent at the far edge of Jensen's western pasture. The tent stood as a glowing spot of unnatural blue among the gray and blue mist of our valley. Hamilton spent three days walking the lower reaches of the mountains. In April, Troublesome Creek runs swift from melting snows. People who live at the far end of the valley carry goods to market on rafts.

On Sunday Hamilton attended church. He joined in hymns, singing in a strained and nearly boyish voice that was most unlike his speaking voice. We know now that either eagerness or tension pinched his song. We enjoyed his presence, thinking him a willing and possibly able man. We have never, in this century, had a convert.

After services matters took an unsettling turn. We stood in

groups after church. Muted sunlight washed across the churchyard, casting pale shadows behind gravestones. Muted breezes
touched spring grass around graves where tulips grew in thick
patches of yellow and red. A few crocus remained.

Hamilton stood among Landstrups and Jensens, as our minister, Jubal Petersen, approached. Hamilton's voice did not carry.
He seemed trying to cooperate with the quiet of Sunday service,
but was awkward with quietness. His large shoulders huddled inside the down jacket. We thought him shy, not manipulative.

"This must be the most peaceful place in the world," he said
to Lars, "although you work very hard." His face was roundish,
like a painting of a Dutch sea captain. Blond hair receded above a
high forehead. His lips were thick, his speech precise. His large
hands were unmarked and carried no callus. The high-laced boots
shone with mink oil. He was somehow aggressive, although he
seemed shy.

"Tibet," Lars said. "I expect Tibetan monasteries are the
most peaceful places in the world. We could probably learn something from them."

"I have means," Hamilton murmured. "What a convenience
it would be if this valley had a water system." He said this with a
straight face, and we tried to receive it with straight faces. "For the
convenience," he said.

"Troublesome Creek is convenient," Lars told him. "That's
why we live beside it."

"For sanitation purposes."

"Our people solved those problems a hundred years ago."
Jubal Petersen joined the group. He looked uneasily toward the
graveyard, then toward hitching rails where horses stood waiting
to pull wagons home. Children ran among the horses, clambered
over wagons and carriages. They laughed and shouted after being
freed from Sunday sermon, but on this Sunday they did not go
near the graveyard.

"Perhaps a stranger might come to belong here," Hamilton
said quietly. "If he required no land and paid his way."

It was a strange statement. It would be difficult to pay one's way around here without working the land. Even our minister is a farmer who earns his family's keep.

"It would make life easier," he said, "if your roads were paved." He looked at the creek and the towpath. "A man could build flatboats engined with a drive on each end. It would be easier to get to church." His voice did not conceal a sort of boyish excitement. Nor did it conceal the notion that he wished to show us his version of salvation.

We've heard it all before. Bring bulldozers to the head of the road. Install electric plants. Bring in oil, gasoline, fire engines, tractors, flush toilets, chainsaws. Life would be easy, then. Idyllic. We've heard it from visitors, and occasionally even from our sons who have just returned. After our sons have been home for a year or two they regain their senses. Still, we had never heard it said with the missionary zeal of Hamilton. He spoke with the fervency of a disciple of 'progress'. His fingers tapped, tapped, tapped at air as he attempted to drive home his points.

"It is true that we work hard," Lars told him. "Whether it's a virtue or not, hard work is the price we pay for the peacefulness you admire." Lars also looked uneasily toward the graveyard. He was a head shorter than Hamilton, but he seemed as tall. He has the blue eyes and thin lips of a Dane, but his voice is always gentle. "You've been here for three days," he said, "and you've heard no sounds of engines. Listen."

Children's voices tinkled joyfully across Sunday silence. Above the mist a hawk circled, and the faded shadow of the hawk slid across fields. The liquid murmur of Troublesome Creek blended beneath the far off crowing of a cock. Horses snuffled, shifted in lightly creaking harness. From the Petersen place a new calf bawled for its mother.

And then silence deepened. For moments even the voices of children seemed muted. From the graveyard came a lack of sound that we had never heard before. The best description would say that it was active silence. Always before, our forefathers have lain passive and tranquil. Their message to us is a message of faith.

Jubal Petersen looked at Lars, then at Hamilton. If the rest of us heard only active silence, it may be that Jubal heard more. "Of all the sins available," he said to Hamilton, "perhaps the sin of pride is most dangerous. Zealousness is often a form of pride." His voice was kind but firm. "We are aware of something happening here that you are not. I must excuse myself."

Jubal turned to the churchyard and walked slowly among the graves. We stood in wonder. Our minister was obviously communing with the dead. His dark-suited figure moved easily, and he occasionally murmured as if answering questions. At first his wrinkled face showed sadness, and then a sort of fear. Jubal is not a man to fear anything, and he especially would not fear our dead.

When he returned he spoke quietly, first to us, and then to Hamilton. "Do not underestimate the eternal power of the human spirit," he told us. To Lars he said, "There's a mystery here, and what I've just said has naught to do with pride." To Hamilton he said, "You are welcome as a guest. Confine yourself to being a guest. If you do that, all will be well."

He raised his hand, not to bless us but to dismiss us. There was plenty of excited talk among the families during the ride home, and during the following week.

During that week madness overcame Hamilton. To his credit he tried to remain respectful, yet his insanity compelled him toward destruction. It seemed that, because he had the power to change things, he could not deny use of the power. We forgive him because of his insanity, but we do not forgive the power that corrupted him.

On Monday morning he folded his tent and disappeared down the road to the outside world. We supposed we were quit of him and were greatly relieved. At the same time we felt loss. Had the man remained among us for a few months his urgency would fade. A good, strong man is never a burden. We knew he was ambitious, did not know that in the world's terms he was rich.

On Friday the distant sound of truck engines came faintly across fields nearest the head of the road. Shortly afterward we heard the chip, chip, chip of a helicopter, and we looked toward the pass where Troublesome Creek begins its slide down the mountain in its rush to the sea. A large silver box hung beneath the helicopter. It proved to be a house trailer. One of the Jorgensen sons went to investigate.

He found Hamilton consulting with surveyors, workmen, and an engineer. The house trailer sat on a ledge and was used as a field office. The men immediately set to work. Through habit, perhaps, they wore hardhats as they climbed along the mountainside at the head of the road. Ancient trees have not survived at that elevation because warm winds sometimes blow in winter. There are many avalanches. Orange hardhats moved through the light-green branches, and surveyors broke or cut young trees to take sights. The snarl of a small chainsaw echoed like a stream of curses.

April is a busy time. Work continued in the fields, but at our backs we felt Troublesome Creek turn from rapid flow to subdued violence. Waters rolled as dark shapes moved just beneath the surface. Occasionally huge, blade-like fins hovered in thin sunlight, then disappeared. This was not a seventh year, a year of flood. Yet Troublesome Creek grew active. Against all custom we quit work two hours before dark. After supper everyone assembled at Sons Of Noah Church.

Families lingered before the church. Soon we would climb the many steps to the church, but at first it seemed necessary to remain clustered before the churchyard. If our ancestors had a say in this matter, as we reverently hoped they did, we wanted ears that would hear.

What we heard caused a strange combination of emotions. We were both soothed and made to fear, although we feared not for ourselves.

It is hard to say whether the voices came from the graves or from Troublesome Creek. The murmuring was vast, as if it rose from creek and fields, from barns, silos, graves; as if it rose with controlled energy from sloping sides of mountains, from the steeple of the church, from the darkening sky. Power rose midst murmurs of peace, a power fantastic, a power that was fabulous.

In our quiet lives there is no equation for such power. There can only be sin in such power. We did not know what we had wrought. The voices assured us that all would be well. The voices were serene with power.

We entered our church. There are many steps, and a railed balcony. One of our sons says it reminds him of a ship's bridge. The church is thriftily made, with clear windows that allow sunlight and starlight.

"You must tell us everything the man said." Jubal talked to Billy Jorgensen, who at fifteen is still awkward, but who can already do a man's work. Billy will soon be known as William, and will take his place among our men.

"Mr. Hamilton has a plan," Billy said quietly. "He schemes a special kind of lodge. I told him about avalanche. He talked about retaining walls."

I am compelled to report that a spirit of fierce and possessive pride overtook our congregation. We watched Billy, listened to his straightforward speech, and each of us no doubt thought of him as our son.

"He plans to sell peace," Billy told us.

Noble thought. But peace cannot be sold, only earned. It developed that Hamilton would treat our way of life as a commodity.

He would build a lodge for the use of those who suffer too much fame. It would be a haven for politicians and generals and movie stars, a place where guests registered only by their first names. He would build a lodge where, if one guest recognized another, it would be the height of discourtesy to acknowledge the other's fame, a place where those who suffered limelight could retreat and for a while become anonymous.

"He means it as a compliment," Billy said. "At least he told me that."

Any man or woman even reasonably sane would understand that Hamilton's plan was a deadly insult. However, insult was not the threat. We have handled insults and misunderstanding since the 1860s.

"He will change what he touches. We must reason with him." Lars is slow to anger, but should he ever turn to anger it would show itself as cold and deliberate fury.

People spoke quickly, agitated, and younger men urged action. Beyond darkened windows wind carried a quick storm of mist, like mighty clouds sweeping the valley. Candles flanked the altar, and candles stood in torcheres beside the aisles. We suddenly felt small and helpless, but not helpless before the ambitions of Hamilton. A torrent of rain began to walk the valley, and rain drummed on the roof of Sons Of Noah Church. The voice of Troublesome Creek deepened. Storm pounded, throwing gales of wind like cannon. We knew what was happening in all the streams and tributaries of the mountains.

"Hamilton and his dreams are removed from our hands," Jubal said, and he was sad. "He is delivered unto other hands." For a moment Jubal looked tenderly at his congregation. "We have lived beside the forces of creation," he said, "and we have underestimated them. We thought, no doubt, that because we are patient, they are patient as well. See to your beasts and your boats. Dawn will light over mighty waters."

Our lanterns gave light unto our feet as we brought beasts to the barns, and yet were we aided by powerful forces. We are accustomed to rain, but on this night where we traveled—to barns, fields, storage sheds—rain only feathered around us. Our swinging lanterns were washed by mist, while everywhere beyond us in the fields and mountains rain pounded like the trump card of heaven.

A clear dawn displayed our well-washed valley where Troublesome Creek ran boiling. Before we ever lifted our eyes toward the end of the valley, we knew that the laws of nature were set aside by nature's God. Troublesome Creek stood three feet above its banks, but it did not flood beyond the banks. It ran like a compressed road of water, standing above the surface of the ground. Great fishes streaked flashes of light. Some of the fishes were dark, but others were cast in luminous colors. Through the years there are more fishes with nearly human eyes. These now dominated the waters. They twisted, dove, then rose to crest in sunlight.

At the end of the valley, the creek no longer discharged down the mountain. It built higher and higher, the voice of water like the sounds of thunder. It rose, as though an ocean were being upended. The turmoil of water echoed like surf. The flood rose as if the great fishes themselves pushed the water, and we could not distinguish crashing waves from the flash of silvery backs. The waters surged here, there, rose and fell in a grand orchestration. The waters sped according to their own designs, or on the commands of unbreachable power.

Water sealed the entrance to the valley, and it steadily rose toward Hamilton's camp. The trucks and house trailer were red and silver dots among the trees, and the wall of water reached forth.

Voices sounded in the distance, but they were not the voices of Hamilton and his men. These voices were ancestral. They were commanding, but serene. They directed the waters, while above the waters sea eagles screamed, dove, beat the air, rose high, only to again dive toward Hamilton's camp, where frightened men scampered like mice.

We clustered beside our church as our young men unhitched horses from carriages. They prepared to ride in an attempt to aid Hamilton. Our young men yelled to each other, and they planned to cast ropes by which men might be drawn to salvation. Our men were desperate in their Godly aim of saving lives.

Jubal stood among us, our rock about which the stream of life swirls. He listened more than he watched, but he also watched our men. "Useless," he muttered, "but of course they must try." He turned to a group of us. "This is *not* about one man with shabby dreams," he muttered. "This is a message to us, and we do well to observe carefully. We'll have to understand the message."

I could see his point. That chaos of water could overwhelm great cities. It did not flow forth simply because of Hamilton, who might be destroyed by a small particle of such enormous energy.

Clouds, of a kind not seen since the creation, formed along ridges of the mountains. There were towering clouds of fire, and equally high clouds of ice; yet the fires did not consume and the ice did not destroy. Fires rumbled upward, darkly smoking, swirling toward the heavens, and sunlight glinted from cascades of shattered ice. Sunlight penetrated black columns of smoke. Light winds swept the valley, interleaving cold and heat, while massive chunks of ice, ripped from glaciers, appeared in Troublesome Creek. Then great winds began to howl, twisting in the high heaven, as if they blew through space from distant stars.

Frightened animals screamed from the safety of barns, and the creek rose steadily until it was a wall of water. The wall stood high, then higher. First it was above our heads, then rapidly grew until it stood above our rooftops, but it still did not flood. Giant trees torn from mountainsides began to twist and turn in Troublesome Creek. Voices rose serenely above the tumult.

I heard the saddened voice of my mother, long dead, and the firm voice of my father, long dead. The ancestry strode invisible among those waters, and we heard the congregated voices of our people. They spoke without hate, only sadness. Yet they commanded the waters.

Hamilton died as men on horses pounded through the valley in an attempt to aid him. He outlasted his cohorts. After all, the surveyors and workmen and engineer were only men doing a job. Their last sight of this world was a rain of glacial ice that killed instantly; and then the bodies were tumbled into the waters and devoured by fishes. Hamilton's death, however, was prolonged.

For a while the creek flowed backward. Then it ceased to flow in any direction and simply stood as a gigantic wall of water. Clouds black as the soul of night stood overhead as lightning crashed, jumped between clouds, illuminated a shadowed landscape that lay beneath volcanic shocks of thunder. Within the wall of water silver flashes streaked, and the flashes echoed human voices. The ancestry rode in those flashes, the eternal human spirit rising to protect—or warn—or teach—we know not which.

Not everything in the creation is beautiful. That which raised its head above the surface, and clasped Hamilton, caused even the bravest of our young men to rein back their horses. Even when the water-form expanded, becoming elongated over half the length of the creek, we could not tell whether it fed with mouths or eyes; for what we took to be mouths were also lidded. They blinked in unaccustomed sunlight, and smoke, and hail. Darkness and light shifted, as if color were liquid, and the creature carried all colors and all darkness.

Hamilton was carried, his round face distorted by screams, just above the surface. The creature of the flood drove the flood, and the flood roared above the tiny voice of Hamilton. This strong man, so filled with pride, but also filled with possibility, thrashed amidst his screams. He called to us, beckoned, and whether he screamed curses or apologies we do not know. His voice garbled with fear, perhaps with repentance, and then his voice was instantly silent. In the enormity of water, the great shape dove into the crevasse, sliding into darkness and the pressure of two thousand feet. Hamilton was only a small spot of color from his expensive clothes as he disappeared into eternal night.

□   □   □

We do not know. We do not know. Mystery surrounds us. We walk in fear of ourselves. To such power we have no right.

With the death of Hamilton the flood receded. Waters sucked into the earth, returned to the crevasse, but no fish were stranded. Troublesome Creek resumed its normal course. Clouds whipped past, then dissolved like echoes. We stood anticipating the eternal promise, the rainbow which stands as sign from the Almighty that He will never again destroy the world by flood. The rainbow appeared, but it brought small comfort.

We returned to our families, our fields, and our beasts. Spring calves romped beside their mothers, and cattle moved fed and content in new grass. The steeple of Sons Of Noah Church rose beside the creek, a loved and familiar silhouette against the surrounding mountains. We have always treasured peace and quiet ways.

Yet we have memories. The first ugly sound of the helicopter, chip, chip, chipping away, like a tiny hatchet attacking a giant tree. We remember the easy confidence of Hamilton, the blindness of his power. He had the money and the equipment and the men that would allow him to alter the very peace he yearned for. He could not deny using his power, nor so, we fear, can we.

Another spring is at hand. Our congregation has met in fear and question for nearly a year. I need explain carefully what troubles us.

The world encroaches. Sometimes, even in this far place, the skies carry a hint of muddy color. On days when winds stand exactly in the mouth of our valley, distant sounds of engines live on the very edge of hearing. More beasts of the field flee here. Deer have always grazed among our cattle, but now the most shy of all large creatures, the elk, gather among our herds. As forests decrease we become sanctuary for wild beasts—bear and cougar and wolves. We control them, these dying generations of animals. We light bonfires in our fields against the wolf. We bear no grievance toward the beasts, who must, after all, pursue life and habitat.

And we bear no grievance against the world of men. After all, perhaps we are 'peculiar' people. Our way is holy to us, but we allow that each man must follow his own path. If that path is one of destruction, then who are we to say it nay? We cannot oppose madness with madness.

But we now understand that Hamilton was a symbol. His death forecasts what may be the death of the world that spawned him. He died in a clash of powers. Against such forces he never had a chance.

Thus do we congregate in fear. Even our children become quiet after service, for children are wise in their ways. They know something is wrong. They sense that we—or our ancestry—or all of us together—control the original, primal energy.

We fear our power. We fear it. Although there is eternal promise that the Creator will not destroy the world by flood, there is no promise that Man will not. We feel tributaries rising in the mountains, and sense the rolling of distant thunder. We feel the rivers of the earth turn quarrelsome. The waters of the earth pulse before our feet. Take heed. Take heed. We feel the oceans bulge.

NOW WE ARE FIFTY

□　□　□

NOW WE ARE FIFTY

THE NIGHT THROB OF FROGS AND CRICKETS LAY LIKE A tumbled blanket across the valley and mixed with the humid vegetable odor of the wet forest. I sat with Frazier in his comfortable house. He remarked that it was still possible to find windowless cabins in these mountains. Not all feuds were dead.

"I never expected it to change." I listened to the pulse of the night. Owls called. Predators and scavengers ranged. In these hills death was direct. I wondered at the compulsion that made Frazier return to this place. In the last few years his poetry has dealt with spirits of dark, voices of shadow, and the gray mystery that intersperses with dappled sunlight on a trail. Such things are the business of poets, but I feared that he was becoming a mystic.

"The mist will rise soon." Frazier stepped to the doorway and looked into the hot Kentucky night. He was framed by the dark. Frazier is tall. His nose hooks and his brows are wide and thick. His face is hollowed and creased. The gray eyes hold either an original clarity or an original madness. They burn bright and sometimes wild. We have been friends all our lives.

Frazier laughed. Erratic. He turned from the doorway to take a chair.

"Now we are all sitting," he said. "You and I sit here. Mink is crouched in his cabin beyond that far ridge. He will be like a night-bound animal. Erickson sits and pilots a broken plane through a tangle of blackberry. A great pilot of affairs was Erickson."

"The man was your friend." He had no right to talk that way about Erickson. I did not need his sarcasm. The situation was more than bad. It was grotesque.

23

A year ago our friend Erickson had checked out on a flight to Ashland in one of his company's planes. He had been engulfed by the forest. Every evidence showed that a man named Mink had killed the injured Erickson. Mink had waited to report the wreckage for a year. He had robbed and mutilated the body. The remains were incomplete. In my briefcase was film I had exposed after a long trek into the mountains.

"Not a friend," Frazier said. "I last saw Erickson in Ashland long ago. It was only for a moment. He was in a hurry."

"And you were not?"

"At the time I was," Frazier said. "Didn't I spend all those years playing the same fool as the rest. Erickson manipulated, you argued law, and I circled poetry like a hawk while wearing a mask of simplicity. These hills, from whence cometh... and yet, I believe it, believe it."

"You complain about what work costs?"

"I'm not complaining about poetry. Where in the hell are my smokes?" He rose to fetch them from the fireplace mantle at the end of the room. "You're wrong," he said. "Erickson had ceased to be a friend. Still, it was strange to see him today. That was a quiet, sober meeting. Erickson was in no hurry."

"You've earned the right to be eccentric, not the right to be cruel."

Frazier ignored me. He returned to the doorway and to the pulsing dark that was filled with death and movement. "It was probably a night like this," he said. "It's almost exactly a year since Erickson went down." He flipped the just lighted cigarette into the darkness. "We were told right away. The sheriff sent a man thirty miles. Name and age and aircraft number. As if that had any special meaning here."

"It had no meaning to Mink."

Frazier tapped at the door frame. Stepped into the dark. Stepped back inside. He wore conventional work clothes of the hills with the shirt sleeves rolled. His forearms were tense.

"It had meaning to Mink," he said. "Erickson was Mink's problem."

"And he solved it with a rifle." I did not try to hide my disgust.

"You're the lawyer. Do you think you have a case?" Frazier turned to gesture to the room which was well furnished and held stacks of current journals, magazines, and books. Recordings were shelved across one end of the room. Work by known painters hung beside sketches by a local artist. The sketches were of drift mouths, blackened faces, and abandoned cabins. Frazier's house was built of native rock and timber. It resembled a small hunting lodge. The differences were subtle. In this house the ceilings were peaked and high. The windows were narrow and heavily draped.

"Identification numbers are out of place here." He gestured again at the books. "Do you think I would be allowed to live in this place if I were very different? I mind my own business." He turned back to the doorway.

"I've been a long time away," I said. "I wouldn't be allowed to live here any more, and when there is murder you don't have to mind your own business. I don't understand you. I don't understand Mink."

". . . that the meek are blessed because they get to stay meek. What is there to understand?"

"You've been here too long." I was convinced of that.

"Don't change the subject. What offends you? The death, or your long wait in the city to confirm the death, or some missing bone. Mink is not that much different from the rest of us."

"Yes he is," I said. "Are you saying you didn't search?"

"We all searched. There are thirty-seven men and boys in this community and all of us searched for four days." Unseen, but in the direction Frazier looked, Hanger Mountain was a ridge rising above slightly lower hills. A trail ran halfway in. It was used for weekly mail delivery by mule.

"We covered every slope beyond this hollow to the three adjacent. We searched until it was a fatality. You could lose a herd of elephants in these hills."

"Something as foreign as a plane?"

"One could crash now within a quarter-mile and you would

not hear. The mist is rising."

"But you did not search Hanger Mountain?"

"The folks from Haw Creek searched that mountain. We trust them."

"Always?"

"In matters such as this, and others not as stupid. And this is not a courtroom. The mist is heavy. Come to the door."

With the proof of death on film the estate could be settled. I was attorney for some of the heirs, and it might be that Frazier would be poet for the crashed plane. I did not want to think of that. I did not want his mist and his bitterness and that humid night.

"You need to be more generous."

"And you more brave. Come to the door."

It was like looking at a black shield. The darkness lay flat as paint, the night voices dim. They were a mutter. A jumble. The stream that during the day filled the clearing with the rush of water now blended with a gurgle, a liquid hint of motion behind the black shield. As my eyes adjusted I saw the mist. It hovered and crawled at short distance. It rose slowly toward the lighted doorway and our feet.

"It will rise faster now," Frazier said. "Let's walk."

"Enjoy yourself."

Frazier turned to me. "You're angry because you're afraid of the night."

"You are the one who is angry."

"Yes," he said. "You are afraid of Mink. Erickson. Twisted metal and twisted lives and skulls that either talk or don't or can't. This is dull. An incident between aging men."

"An incident of murder."

"Only an incident that's a little mysterious. Erickson would have understood."

"There's no mystery," I said. "The plane crashed and Mink took all he could get and then waited to see if a reward would be offered. So Erickson's affairs are delayed for a year."

"Erickson attends to his affairs," Frazier said. "He is doing it now. Doing the only business he has left."

This sullen, intellectual son of a bitch. He was asking to do battle. Arrogance. My mind is as good as his.

"And you are not afraid?"

"No," he said. "Beleaguered. You people will not leave us alone. You will not leave the hills alone. Erickson helped destroy these hills with his mining. You and your precious business." He stepped through the black shield and into the night.

Without him I would be lost within a hundred feet. Between his mood and mine it would be crazy to make myself dependent on Frazier. I walked the length of the room to sit by the fireplace, which was clean and gray from fires of the half-dozen winters Frazier has lived here. The mist was beyond the heavy drapes. The voices of frogs and the mutter of the stream were like a murmur of the mist. The night was hot and wet but I felt almost cold.

Murder. I hate this land where we were raised. It was my old acquaintance with Frazier that brought me back. Ordinarily we would have sent a younger man.

Erickson had hated this place. It is dark, wet, hot, violent. Erickson's life was spent trying to deal with the waywardness of boondocks Kentucky.

Murder. When Erickson checked in missing, it caused the interlocked directorships of three coal corporations to start earning their pay. No one knew this place like Erickson. Erickson could talk to men who wear overalls and do business while standing in small-town streets. When Erickson disappeared I had written to Frazier. He had written back and told me to stay away.

The heirs became impatient and offered a five-thousand-dollar reward. The results were on film.

"A hundred dollars would have gotten the same result." Frazier said that on the morning two days ago. On that morning we began our trek in to view the crash. A guide walked ahead of us. Silent. Although Frazier owned a mule he said that no suitable mules were available. The silent guide carried a machete.

Along the trail were deep slits in the rock where coal seams had been entered. They were good seams.

"They still risk their lives for that," I said. People around here have always scrabbled free coal. Sunlight reached toward the black veins. The bracing props were stout, but this had nothing to do with mining. Even from the trail we could see fallen slate.

"They do not have much money," Frazier said.

The trail branched down through a stream bed bridged by logs, and then wound across the base of the first mountain. Laurel grew like trees. Shrubbery and sapling growth was brushed greener by humidity. It would be a full day's hike.

In a mile the trail narrowed and in five miles it was an overgrown footpath. Under foot was the give and slight backward pressure of deep moisture. Our guide shouldered through brush. Silent and sullen. Since I arrived I had spoken to no one but Frazier. The suspicion of these hills. It is redneck, hot, hillbilly, and righteous.

"There is a mixture of spirits in these hills." Frazier was musing to himself. "The Cherokees left some, for they were an ambitious people with emissaries north and south. The Scots Presbyterians brought some along, and the first evangelicals invented some."

I said nothing. He did not want conversation.

"Spirits of mist, thunder, wind and spirits of the dark." He laughed, low, brittle. The man ahead slashed at blackberry. The trail rose and then again descended. It was hot and getting hotter.

"Spirits of the dark," Frazier said. "Well, and we are getting old, and most mystery is only a contrivance." There was a sudden flurry ahead. A kick, the sound of a machete striking the forest floor, a hush.

"Stand still," Frazier said. "There's often a nest of them."

The guide pushed at foliage with the machete. He kicked the brush. Then he motioned us forward. Blood lay on the trail, and the pieces of a hacked snake.

"Always where it's low and wet," Frazier said. The reptilian blood was almost black on the humus. The head was split, the body chopped. Though he walked heavily our guide had been swift.

We walked. After the fourth hour my body passed from

revulsion to acceptance and the trek was mechanical. Mine is a good body. Even under pressure I could depend on my movements. Part of it comes from early training. Erickson and Frazier and I had all been trained to movement and the use of tools when we were young. It was not until we arrived and met Mink that it occurred to me how much Frazier resembled Erickson and how much I resembled both of them.

There are hill people and there are sorry people. Between the two there is as much difference as between a stump preacher and a theologian.

Mink was well named. I have known a thousand like him. Sly, shifty, and with long teeth. He moved with no dignity of age or experience. His clothes and cabin stank. The permanent coal dust that gets into the skin of miners circled his eyes; and his eyes were dull and clouded and suspicious. His gaze only seemed vacant. He looked more like a dying raccoon. One that could still bite.

His shack was empty but there was the mark of a woman and children. Pictures had been clipped from catalogs and religious magazines. A worn doll was tossed in a corner. The family was away visiting. They would return when we left.

"Let's unroll the sleeping bags outside," I said.

"Mosquitoes," Frazier told me. His voice carried a warning I did not understand.

We ate from our packs and lay bundled on the floor. The trek in had been exhausting. There would still be inspection of the wreckage and the trek out. The coroner was old, Frazier told me. When the wreck was more than hearsay a deputy would bring the body out by helicopter. The inquest was a rubber stamp.

Two days of heat and fatigue. Now I sat in Frazier's long, low timbered room and stared at the shield of dark. To have to consider murder after two days of fatigue and fear and wreckage.

The wings had sheared from the plane and were tossed far enough that they did not burn. The identification numbers, white on the red wings, were like remote signals from a space of trees. The forest was dull in late summer. The pines held no gloss. Deciduous trees were chewed and ragged from August storms and insects. The fuselage lay on its side and was half-gutted by fire. I had not wanted to do the necessary work because it was terrible, and because I had known the man.

Where steel was exposed there was rust, and the aluminum skin curled from fire. I watched twisted metal and tried to keep my hands from trembling. A year's accumulation of dirt lay in tiny pockets and waves of metal. The engine twisted away from the cockpit. I looked, tried to speak, motioned to Frazier.

"No animal would do this." I turned to check the forest. Where was Mink? I felt the place between my shoulders where a bullet might enter, turned, felt the same place in my chest.

"Spirits of the dark," Frazier muttered. "No animal could."

"Where is he?"

"Keep working. Lawyers don't get hysterics."

There had been only silence, and the silence lasted all through the long trek back. Now I sat in Frazier's living room, my thoughts scattered. Mink would get by with it. There was no love here for Erickson. There was no proof that a scavenger had not gotten to the body. Of course, Mink was stupid. He would betray himself if questioned. But who would bring him out unless there was some old grudge.

How stupid was he? I rose from the chair. Had he thought it over in his dull-minded, murderer's way and thought of his danger? Had he followed me? I know these people.

The muffled sounds of the night pulsed. The door stood open to the darkness, and the black shield seemed to move. The dark soul of the night. The dark heart of these people who have always bred revenge and killers. There was no mystery here. There was only fear and greed and violence.

I wanted to call to Frazier and stepped toward the doorway. Then I stopped. He had said that he was like them. The night was a glowering spirit of fear. It was the only spirit of this place.

Terror passed slowly. By the time Frazier returned I felt under control. Resignation replaced fear.

When he stepped from the dark it was like the appearance of a specter. His hair and face and clothing were shining with mist.

He brushed at his sleeves. His shirt was damp and showed the mark of his hand.

"Why do you defend Mink?"

"I defend no one," he said. "That's in your line."

"I defend what I can understand."

"Then understand this."

"Impossible."

"No," Frazier said, "it's possible. You have been away too long. If you were in a foreign country you would be more generous, more understanding. Man, this is not Madrid or Paris. These are the hills."

"Murder is murder."

"Tell Erickson about it." He crossed the room to choose a recording. The room was designed for music, the measured address of an orchestra perfectly transmitted. One did not think of volume. The room lived in music, and the music was surely Bach. Frazier walked the length of the room to sit by the cold fireplace.

I waited for one more lecture or protest. This had been going on most of my life. It would be better for both of us if we had never been friends.

"Erickson may have been hurt," Frazier said. "Forget what's missing because Mink hid some bone broken by his bullet. It's twenty miles from anywhere on Hanger Mountain, at least two days to a doctor."

"But to kill . . ."

"Sometimes around here a dog gets snake bit. We shoot it quick."

"And to rob."

"Dammit, how do you know? He's ignorant and was afraid and had to try to burn the plane, but Mink is a decent man. At least as decent as the rest."

"And he did not report."

"Yes," Frazier said. "That's what really bothers you. On the other hand, why do you intrude with your five thousand dollars and pure intentions?" He leaned back, stretched his long legs and waited. The music surrounded us. I remained silent to force him to speak.

"Erickson was dead when he took the first course in engineering at that cow college," Frazier said. "He was dead the first time he spent ten cents on mineral rights."

"All three of us went to that college."

"And all three of us chose how we would die." There was a rush of music. "Illusions," he said. "Such a splendid choice of illusions, and so we made our choices."

"We're talking about Mink."

"It's dark out there." Frazier motioned to the now-closed door. "Mink is not much different, and most of the darkness is only natural darkness. It cares nothing for our concerns, law, poetry, business, what does it matter?"

"My friend..."

"Yes," he said, "but the rest... it's the darkness of the mind. Toy monkeys on a stick. A dime a jump if you jump high." He broke off and sat watching me with neither judgment or affection.

"You remember when I came here," he said presently. "All of you, my friends, cautioned me against being a fool. You cautioned me. Yet, you have known me longest. You know how high I climbed my stick, did my tumbles, tipped my hat and mumbled and grimaced out there." He motioned to the closed door.

"You are famous."

"Enough to choose. I spend my time with a mule, a cow, a few chickens and a small garden. I occupy myself sorting Presbyterian ghosts, spirits, devils and haunts that are all illusory because they cloud the few real mysteries of these hills. My death is on my face, wrinkled, hawkish, and I feed my beasts and listen to *The Art of the Fugue*."

"Are you dying?"

"Yes. Listen. Erickson was no different. I speak of dying. All of us, all of our lives tied to these hills. We left because our fathers had jobs in the city. Erickson became rich, I became famous, and you...."

"Have done my job."

"...have also chosen."

"And Mink could not choose? Pity is a poor thing."

"And waste is a lousy thing, but you are right about pity. Mink spent his life in the mines."

"Which belonged to Erickson. You are getting childish. Are you really dying?"

"Hell, the mines belong to whoever owns mines, and I am getting angry. We do not speak of equity or irony. The whole lot of us are only representative props in a two-bit melodrama. By God!" His lips were drawn and white.

"Props," he said. "Whatever you do, whoever we are, but the props fall because of the human heart... Mink's work was harsh work."

"I don't want to feed your anger," I told him, "but everyone works and gets old."

"Yes. Except Mink had no pretense about work or the hills. We were trapped in illusion. Trapped in the immemorial darkness that will always be one of the true mysteries." He paused. Glanced at the closed door. "Your life was worth the price of a bullet awhile ago. You were vulnerable. No pretense. No illusion. I sat beneath a poplar and watched. Had you come here for the right reason..." Frazier stood, but did not walk to the record shelves. He crossed the open room to the kitchen area and began to brew tea from a local herb. With the door closed the night sounds were muted but still present. For a moment the room seemed like a lighted cave.

"This whole matter was none of our affair," he said. "Erickson intruded. He had no right to be here with those intentions and his pitiful business. He had no right to come sailing over Mink. He had no right to crash on Mink's place and leave wreckage to plague another man. Will the concerned heirs pay to have that junk removed? Erickson's last intrusion on Mink was just one of a thousand."

"What in the hell are you preaching?" I felt that he really must be dying and raving in the face of it.

"You don't see it," he said. "Forget it. But, man, you are alien. You have interfered and have no right to interfere further. Come on a true visit, or send me your letters, but stay away from these hills with your intrusions. This tea is always a little bitter."

"As bitter as the host?"

"Even now," Frazier said, "you intrude on Mink. You are going to give him money."

"Or press charges."

"Try to understand."

I felt that I should be angry and was not. The murmur of the night lay just beyond the heavy drapes. I could hear it, restless, throbbing and certain.

"The wreck looks worse than it was. Maybe Erickson was hurt. Maybe he was only unconscious." Frazier sipped at his tea. "There is no way to know what Erickson thought, and there is no way to know what Mink thought because his mind is heavy and dead and he would not remember. He would tell you that Erickson was snake bit, and around here that is a cliché."

"The man is an animal."

"The man has become an animal, now an animal with five thousand dollars."

"You object to the money?"

"The immemorial darkness," Frazier said. "Already folks call it blood money. They would not lend a mule to help in the matter. I would not myself. Mink might have lived in that hollow for the rest of his life, and been buried by his children. Predict his future now? I would not dare." Frazier motioned to the delicate porcelain cup that was as strange in this place as a mule would be in a law office.

"My anger passes," he said. "When I die the people here will bury me. Then, without discussing it, they will divide the plunder. I have made provisions for the manuscripts and a few of the books."

"What does that have to do with anything?"

"Everything. It's what remains from all the things that happen, and which we believe and which have no meaning. Are you so layered with illusion that you do not believe in revenge, which is another of the true mysteries. Man, I'm not just talking about the spirit of these hills."

". . . that they will destroy or steal your property?"

"That Erickson had his, I have had mine and you are engaged in yours. It's sodden revenge. That's all. There is no heat in it. We are old."

"Maybe you are."

"We are old. Old as revenge."

"And you are a fool," I said. "I do my job."

"Yes, yes, and well, there is the Bach. Sometimes, even now, there is poetry. Around here people can sing very sweet. They do that. Some make their own musical instruments. There are new ways to mine and new ways to build airplanes. The quality of rifles improves each year from Army surplus. I listen to the Bach, walk through the natural darkness, and protest against intrusion. Sometimes when there is a gray dawn the forest and pasture are silver when I walk down to feed the mule, and those dawns always happen in winter. The chickens are safe behind wire fences because the valley runs with hounds and foxes."

He looked at me and his face was creased, gaunt, shadowed in the low light and filled with his particular madness. "You leave in the morning," he told me. "File your report, send Mink the money, ignore the rest. It is none of your business." He walked to the door.

"Will you stay?"

"Here," he said. "Yes, right here, but for now I go to check on the beasts." He opened the door, stepped through the black shield and was engulfed. I saw him no more that night and he was uncommunicative in the morning.

I left in a dawn that promised high humidity and heat. We rode in Frazier's old car along broken road. My driver was yet another silent man from the community. We bumped along and connected with a state road. I was carried to Ashland.

My plane flew over mountains that were like waves of green light and glaring heat. They shone in sunshine and reflected the shadow of the plane. The shadow ran beneath the left wing and appeared and disappeared below us. Cuts between the mountains, hollows and ravines, the dark gullies and slashes on the landscape swallowed the shadow only to throw it onto the next bright mountain top. The shadow traveled like a gray imp, a faded demon, and for those stretches where the landscape was altered it was nearly invisible. Erickson had been dead for a year. Frazier was dying in his chosen place and time and manner, and I was responsible for the affairs of others . . . but damn him, to be told that I had no right to be here.

The pilot banked above a river and followed it north. The shadow ran beneath us and only a little forward. It pointed toward the world I had chosen.

All right. Maybe the son of a bitch was correct in his madness. I would respect it enough to respect his wish about Mink: and let him be correct. It was his world that was helpless, not mine. But he still had no right to tell me that I had no right to be here.

RESURRECTION

□ □ □

RESURRECTION

TAKE THE PATH BEHIND THE KINGDOM HALL, THE PATH circling back into blackberry bushes and scrub and trees—where on most mornings gray mist hangs in the tops of young fir and old madrona—and there is a clearing where most evenings a solitary man talks with dead neighbors. His name is Em, he is sixty. He always has a white dog with him. Some folks say he has two.

Lona-Anne-Marie is the only one who knows all Em's movements. Lona-Anne-Marie is stove up with eighty years, and with thirty years of doorbelling, and tracts, and waiting the awful coming of a resurrecting God. She lives in a wonderland of faith. The waiting makes her beautiful. She is wrinkled and tiny and clothed in repaired things bought for a quarter at thrift shops. She can walk a little, but mostly she sits in her kitchen and watches the neighborhood. When summer sun is vague in this Pacific Northwest mist, it falls in silverish-yellow pebbles across the roof of Kingdom Hall. It isn't hard to imagine the Angel Gabriel standing astride the roof. Even we who have our doubts can think him there.

"The world is getting old and Em is aging," Lona-Anne-Marie explains. "The world is holding up pretty well, all things considered."

Behind the Kingdom Hall, and dug in beneath sheltering blackberries, lies a private cemetery. Somebody's people were buried in vague and unremembered graves: John, another John, Sarah, Esther, Timothy. The whole business sits on a bluff; and, off to the left, deer and raccoon and a black bear inhabit a deep ravine that angles down to the salt water of Puget Sound. Before young trees grew, before blackberries covered them over, those five graves looked eastward at the Sound, like planted sailors pointing boots toward the sea. A homestead once stood where now stands a broken chimney. The people died of illness. Madrona trees seeded. Some of the madrona are seventy or eighty years; hard to tell. Madrona doesn't grow like other trees. You can't count the rings.

Our neighborhood is small. A little block of apartments anchors the head of the street. People move in, then move out. Clunkity cars with mattresses strapped to roofs arrive and leave like aging gypsies. The cars are many-colored, like Joseph's coat frayed after years in one or another desert. Each time the paper mill hires or fires, people reshuffle. Faces of school children are exchanged for other schoolish faces. Beside the apartments sits Nancy's prim and puffy house with yellow shutters. The children call her 'the mean lady', and children know.

"Nancy has such a pretty name," Lona-Anne-Marie ponders, sometimes to Nancy. "A body has to wonder what went wrong."

Across from Nancy's sits the ramshackle house of Jim and Lois, although Jim now lives at Odd Fellows Cemetery; he's dead these three years. Winter, summer, every week, Lois carries flowers to his grave. The ramshackle is crowded with junk on three floors. Jim collected stuff. Beside Nancy's house is the smallest house in the neighborhood, which is Lona-Anne-Marie's, and beside that, a vacant lot where a poetic lady from the apartments in years past strowed some seed. The lot is all grass and weeds and the lady's poppies, purple and red and orange and white.

Em's house sits across from Lona-Anne-Marie. Beside Em sits the nice little place with Pete and Mona. They're retired. Then comes two more vacant lots. Kingdom Hall comes at the end of the street. Beyond the Hall's parking lot there is nothing but trees, and the private cemetery; and, when the wind is wrong, the mill's smell.

"Em is learning something about graves," Lona-Anne-Marie explains, sometimes to Em. Em visits her when he's not working. "Em is learning that between the living and the dead there ain't no difference." Lona-Anne-Marie chuckles, like she was the only snapdragon in a bed of asparagus. We figure Lona-Anne-Marie can be so sure because she has eternity locked. She likes patched blue housedresses, red sweaters, the coming rebirth of the world, and garage sales. She likes children from the apartments, and she likes the overweight and worried mothers who come looking for kids. Lona-Anne-Marie's hair is whiter than Em's dog. That's white.

"Are we old and wise," Pete says, "or only old?"

"Ask me stuff like that, I'm gonna Witness." For Lona-Anne-Marie wisdom belongs somewhere in the heavens. It may descend to earth on Sunday mornings.

Through the neighborhood conversation flows. What's said to Em is later heard by Pete. Lois talks to Lona-Anne-Marie, then Nancy hears. Lona-Anne-Marie tells Nancy to stop acting mulish. About that, Mona hears. We don't talk behind the others' backs. Talk circulates like a family.

When his first dog died Em supposed himself in many ways a fool. Nancy agreed. Lona-Anne-Marie said things would mend. Pete was sympathetic. Mona worried. Lois is youngest, being fifty-eight. She baked pies.

It was not a dog that should have been in business. He was happy-go-sloppy, a dog that rode in Em's old truck. Em peddles. He sells and trades: chainsaw parts and magazines. Rope and tack and tools and books and notions. The truck sags with wants and needs and used up dreams. It carries useful stuff and other people's junk. Before Jim died, a lot of trading went on between Jim and Em.

That dog, and Em, and truck made quite a picture. The truck is more-or-less a Ford, but improved. Used to be a milk truck painted green. Funny color for a milk truck. Em is skinny and hawk-nosed, frowzy like the truck. He wears work clothes. The dog was shiny white, a curly tail. They held conversations, people heard. Em never even sings in church, but in that truck he sang a monotone. The dog would whine and woof. Em is modest. He never bragged except about the dog. He claimed he traded out a five-buck Chevy carb. "Best five-dollar dog I ever owned," he'd say, and he was lying.

It was the *only* dog he'd ever owned. Like a fool, he guessed it to live forever. Inexperience can hurt.

"How can people live when they lose children," Em asked Lona-Anne-Marie. "Because this was just my dog and I can't stand it."

"Depends on who does the losing," Lona-Anne-Marie told him. "Creation's perfect, people ain't."

"I don't know what that means."

"Let's hope you never do," Lona-Anne-Marie told him. "I never met a man so like a child."

After burying the dog beneath an apple tree, Em took up playing pool. He hung around the bars.

"He'll bring a floozy home. Expect that next." Nancy is iron-haired and skinny, but chesty. Claims nobody sees her nicest parts. This shocks Mona, tickles Lois. Lois kind of slid while Jim was dying. Got overweight. A florid smile with painful eyes. She drinks a little. Mona dyes her long hair brown. It looks nice. Tiny women don't much show their age.

"It's like he's still around," Em said to Lona-Anne-Marie. "Like he don't want to leave . . . all in my mind, of course."

"Don't count on it. You think the world's that simple?"

"It always was before," Em said. "I may retire. I'll get myself a cat and settle down. Learn to fly a rocking chair."

"Don't do it," Pete told Em when word got round. "It only *sounds* like fun." Pete is tall and sixty-eight, skinny and bald-headed. He fished for a living. Now he fixes and refixes on his house. The way that man can go through paint. Gallons.

Em went through a phase. Talking to his dog. With morning mist above the Kingdom Hall, Em walked the path that leads down to the graves. The dog went with him. Invisible, of course. "C'mon, mutt-dog," Em would say, and off the two walked among the trees.

"He wants a padded cell." Nancy claimed that Em was going nuts.

"He wants a woman," Lois said.

"And that's the man who says he'll get a cat? He wants

another dog." The paper comes out once a week. Mona started reading classifieds.

"He's got a dog," Lona-Anne-Marie told Mona. "Tarry awhile on those puppy ads."

"He wants to give up pool and get to work." Pete figured Nancy was close to being right. He figured Em's brains were moon-scuffed. "I've seen ten-year-olds with better sense."

"I've lost people who I didn't miss as much," Em confided to Lona-Anne-Marie. "Pretending makes it better though." Em went back to work. Each morning when he climbed into his truck, he held the door until the dog jumped in. The whole thing looked natural. Lois claimed she nearly saw the dog.

"If that's the way to handle grief I'm going to try," Lois told Lona-Anne-Marie. "I'll walk through all my rooms and talk to Jim."

"There goes the neighborhood," Pete said when he was told. "This place is gonna be a loony bin."

"The preacher says that dogs don't have a soul," Em told Lona-Anne-Marie. "I think of changing churches."

"It's what you get for being Methodist."

Lois' health improved. She cut back on wine. She no longer carried flowers to Jim's grave. Autumn came with autumn rains. The path behind the Kingdom Hall became a swamp. Fat blackberries of August turned to September blue and purple pulp, while mist ran rivers through the stand of trees. We fed our woodstoves, looked toward the rain; salvation. Boot and slicker weather. Folks who love the sun don't like it here. We get a lot of wet. We get a lot of winter.

Em still walked his dog along the path. Then Jim and Lois joined them. Three people and a dancing dog, the living and the dead.

"It's getting out of hand," Pete said to Nancy.

"Maybe so," said Lona-Anne-Marie, "but Lois has quit drinkin'." Lona-Anne-Marie is rarely puzzled. When resurrection's certain, not much else is going to fool you. Still, Lona-Anne-Marie was thinking. The rebirth of the world seemed out of kilter.

Em bought a female pup with pedigree. "Because males fight," he said to Lois. "I want them to be friends."

"For what that mutt cost," Pete said, "he could of paid the taxes on his house."

The rains swept in across the western range, rains bred in Russia, the Gulf of Alaska; sou'westers coming from Japan. The roof on Kingdom Hall sat glazed and black. Em turned to motherhood and so did we.

"We're acting silly." Lona-Anne-Marie was gratified. "A man of sixty ain't too old to learn." She watched Em's patience as he trained the pup. She boiled soup bones and watched as Em, and Jim, took walks with the two dogs.

"She'll get pneumonia," Nancy said, "that's sure. They come in cold and wet." She searched her attic, found a blanket. She and Lois made the pup a bed.

Pete built a doghouse. "Big enough for *one,*" he pointed out.

"I look to the redemption of the world. Not this. Right now I've got a mare's nest." Lona-Anne-Marie was always sure a resurrecting God would sweep the sky and make things new. For thirty years since her conversion she's passed out tracts.

"Jim don't explain why he's returned. Might be he can't. And I don't care." Lois started working on her weight. "I used to be nice looking."

"He really likes her." Em told everyone about his dogs. "It's going to work out fine."

"I think Em did just right, and so does Jim." Lois' eyes were nowhere near as painful. "I know you think it's crazy," she told Mona.

"I don't know what to think. There's something to it." Mona started greeting Jim, when Jim and Lois took their morning walk. It like to drove Pete wild.

"I almost, just about, can see him," Mona said. "Maybe they're not crazy."

"I don't care much for kids. I do like dogs." Nancy got maternal. She swore that Em was going to ruin the pup.

"She seems to pee a lot," Em said.

"She's got a baby bladder." Nancy went downtown, and bought a book on how to train your dog.

"How to *ruin* your dog," Pete said. "They've got that little girl downright confused."

"Maybe so," said Lona-Anne-Marie, "and maybe not. Watch where she *doesn't* jump, watch where she does."

"There's no predictin' what a pup will do." Pete watched close. The pup seemed romping with another dog. When Jim and Lois went along with Em, the pup seemed with three people. She danced in front of Jim; like he took space. She didn't run across his space.

"It's mass delusion," Pete explained. "The neighborhood is nuts, and so's my wife. I've lived beside that woman forty years. I think I've lost my mind."

"Folks get lonesome," Nancy said. "We're old. If everybody's happy why complain? The world don't care for old folks anyway. We get to act as silly as we please." Nancy didn't give a thought for Jim. She only walked along to bother Pete.

On Sunday mornings at the Kingdom Hall folks come and go like businessmen at lunch. They chomp an hour's message, then leave. Used to be, when church was over folks would stand around. They'd talk and gas and gossip, swap the news. Girls would flirt with boys, and boys would blush. There was no helter-skelter.

On Sunday mornings Lona-Anne-Marie can almost always walk to Kingdom Hall. Unless the weather's awful, or unless her rheumatism bends her. On such days, Em or Pete walks with her. They don't stay. They pick her up when services are done.

One day she walked with Jim. People took no notice. Except the people in the neighborhood. Lona-Anne-Marie leaned on Jim's arm. Her white hair puffed beneath a mended scarf. Her red coat was a thrift store hand-me-down.

"That tears it," Pete said. "I must be missin' something."

"My dog has caused the resurrection of the world." Em spoke to Lois. "Don't tell nobody yet. He died and didn't want to leave.

I take no credit."

Used to be that things weren't lonesome. When church let out the old folks stood around, and counted blessings. They had families, they had friends. They knew about each other back to Adam. Some were even feuding.

"It don't pay to fret about the past. I've nary chick nor child to plague me. I think about the future." Lona-Anne-Marie was optimistic. If resurrection's certain, folks can plan. "It's just," said Lona-Anne-Marie, "redemption should be fancy. I thought the skies would open."

The pup grew winter fur. Along the path behind the Kingdom Hall, and on the bluff where the old chimney rose, someone cut young trees. We heard the axe-chunks carried by the wind. Winter brings us freezing rain. Our world is covered with transparent glaze.

"John's resurrected," Em explained. "His whole family. Those five graves behind the Kingdom Hall. John's putting up a cabin. John Jr.'s helping; nice young man. Esther's just a little girl, and Tim is ten. Sarah can't be more than thirty-five. Folks married younger eighty years ago." Em told all this to Pete and Jim while rummaging his truck. "I've got some stuff they're going to need. Cooking pots and such. They gotta have a stove." He turned to Jim. "I'll bet you've got a couple in your shed."

"I must be gettin' old," Pete said, "I'm tired. This disbelieving wears a fella down." The sound of axe-chunks carried from the bluff. "It won't be up to code," Pete said. "There's no permit. The sheriff's gonna come and raise some hell."

"We're past the time of sheriffs, I expect." Jim seemed certain-sure. "Woodstoves weigh a lot. We'll have to pack it down in parts. Bolt it back together on the site."

"Oh, Lord," Pete said, "I just now heard Jim's voice. Now *everybody's* crazy."

Used to be, miracles abounded. Every family had at least one tale, of someone on the far side of death's door that death tossed back. Or maybe angels cruised the neighborhoods. There was a time when faith moved mountains. Pete was old enough to recollect.

"I'd ought to call the sheriff. Get this done." Nancy can be mulish. The minute Pete began to talk to Jim, Nancy balked. Her iron-gray hair looked like a puff of mist as she peered from her windows. When Em and Jim and Lois and the dogs went walking down behind the Kingdom Hall, Nancy stayed at home. "I've been playing this just like a game. Never took it serious."

"Pipe dreams come from smoke. I see no smoke." Lona-Anne-Marie cleaned house. She washed her windows, polished up her stove. "I ain't seen Pete so lively in awhile. He's finally taking interest. It's making Mona happy."

Lona-Anne-Marie washed curtains. The rebirth of the world would find her tidy. She had few words about the resurrection. "It had to happen sometime. Why not now? I've been predictin' it."

When woodsmoke rose behind the Kingdom Hall the sheriff came. Webster Smith ("Call me Web") is sheriff. He's friendly when election comes around. "There's law and folks," he says, and what he means is comfort lies in balancing the two. Web does like comfort.

"I'm not so young myself," Web said to Pete. He stood beside his car and watched the trees. Dead poppies straggled in the vacant lot, while off a-ways, two playing children looked like bouncing toys.

"Old folks imagine things. I ought to know. Try sittin' in a car night after night. Looking out for drunks." Web had walked the path, looked at the site. Nancy got so bothered she'd joined Pete. They'd waited side by side until Web got back. Web is not bad-looking, tall and built in chunky squares.

"What did you see?" Nancy frets at things, won't let them go. She's not above some flirting. Web has always been a ladies' man.

"A cabin built by axe. It's some poor duffer. Riding out the winter. Don't own a chainsaw, even."

"I'd just as leave this didn't get around. I think there's something to it." Pete winked at Jim, who only Pete could see. From up the path behind the Kingdom Hall Em walked with his two dogs.

"The folks at Kingdom Hall made no complaint. The land belongs to them. Come spring the guy will move along. Meanwhile, I won't roust him." Web had got distracted. Nancy'd pulled her shoulders back. It made her front stick out.

"None of us has got that many years." Web looked at Kingdom Hall like he was tired. "We mix up fact and memory. These days I spend a lot of time remembering my folks." Web looked where Em was coming from the trees. "I heard he bought a high-price pup. Why's he need two dogs?"

"Sweet loving God," said Nancy. Then she drooped her shoulders.

The sum of it is John and Sarah stayed, together with their kids. They feared hard times. It isn't easy, after eighty years, to make a living. They were raised with horses, not with cars; but everybody helped.

On Sundays, going to the Kingdom Hall, folks drove past and sort of looked confused. They'd wave to Pete and Em, and Em's two dogs, or maybe one. When spring rains came, a few of them began to wave at Jim.

"I got to guess," said Lona-Anne-Marie, "the skies will open soon."

In spring the rain is constant. It walks across the mountains and the Sound. It floods our gardens and the vacant lots. Hard to work the ground, the earth gets soggy. The roof of Kingdom Hall grows moss. The moss is softly green. It burns away come summer.

The pup grew to a dog and Em was thinking. "It's old folks make this happen," he told Jim. "Lona-Anne-Marie knew all along. The living and the dead are all the same. I'll get it studied out."

"Faith don't amount to squat," Pete said to Em. "Unless you're stuck with facts. Then there's something to it."

"Maybe we all died," said Em, "and none of us took notice."

In May the rains turn warm and start to thin. Our world is green. New growth tips the firs. The pines grow whitish candles. The roof of Kingdom Hall looks like a lake, reflecting trees.

"It comes from being lonesome," Em told Jim. "I'd guess it's more than that, but there's a start."

"It's getting ticklish down at Kingdom Hall." Lona-Anne-Marie still went to church. "Some folks say 'yes', and some say 'no'. Can't blame 'em much. A quiet resurrection's real surprising." Lona-Anne-Marie was feeling spry. When kids from the apartments came around, she gave them little parties.

"It's kind of cute," said Nancy. "Folks from Kingdom Hall talk resurrection. Then it comes and they don't see it. I guess it don't amount to much."

"It's having *everything,* plus lonesome." Em told Nancy, then told Pete. "Youngsters couldn't do it. Been listening to the preachers sixty years. It took my dog to teach me."

When John and Sarah took their kids to church, the congregation put its cares aside. Redemption maybe—maybe not—but here were folks who had to make a crop. The elders took a vote. They had a man come in. Tractored up the vacant lots. They bought hand tools and seed.

"I know now how it works," Em said to Pete. "Dead folks are all around."

Young folks have needs, Em claims. When they get lonesome they just chase their tails. They do those things young people have to do. Em says the resurrection always was, has always been. It just takes folks who have no wants, but feel the pain of lonesome. Em claims the skies won't open.

Lona-Anne-Marie believes they will. She waits and watches. In the vacant lots, the poppies have give way to scarlet runner beans. John and Sarah seem to have the touch. Their crop is thrifty.

John thinks Em is right; Jim isn't sure. The rest of us are waiting. When summer dawns throw silver light in patches through the trees, we watch the sky. The roof of Kingdom Hall is pebbled gold, not much has changed. On Sunday mornings folks pass to and fro. They wave and go their ways when services are done. The neighborhood falls quiet, save for children's play, while in the parking lot of Kingdom Hall two white dogs dance, or sniff at oil spots where the cars were parked.

TINKER

□ □ □

TINKER

THERE WERE TROUBLED AUGUSTS ONCE, BACK WHEN OUR grandmothers were still alive, and when dog days panted slowly toward busy Septembers. Narrow roads overlaid old Indian trails, cutting through squared-off fields. The roads were white gravel. In midwest August dawns, the roads turned orange. Later in the day, they flowed like strips of light between green and yellow crops. Along these roads the tinker followed his trade.

We would see his wagon a mile off. Children began to holler. Women on the farm, mothers and grandmothers and cousins, exchanged glad looks behind the backs of any men who happened to be around. The tinker was a ladies' man, but not in the usual sense.

This was the time of the Great Depression. Farms were flattened. People were broke. Gasoline was used only for the tractor, or, once a week, taking the Ford to town. In those days horses were not spoiled little darlings. They worked the same as everyone else. Our people lived on hope, religion, the kitchen garden, a few slaughtered swine; and chicken after chicken after chicken. Even now, fifty years later, I cannot look a roasting hen in the eye.

The tinker had a regular route through the county. We saw him twice a year. Most tinkers were older men, but this one was middling young. My mother claimed he was a gypsy, my grandmother claimed him Italian, and the menfolk claimed him an Indian/mulatto who was after someone's white daughter. But, I'd best explain about tinkers. In today's throw-away world they are extinct.

The tinker's wagon was a repair shop on wheels. It resembled a cross-breed between farm wagon and Conestoga, but light enough for hauling by two horses. It carried torches for brazing, patches of sheet metal, patches of copper. It held soles for shoes, and grinders for knives and scissors. It was a-clank with cooking pans hanging along its sides. The tinker repaired worn pots, glued broken china so skillfully one could hardly find the crack, fixed stalled clocks; in fact, repaired anything that required a fine hand. This tinker also repaired worn dreams. That was the seat of his trouble. And ours.

I remember all this, not only through the eyes of a child, but through the eyes of a historian. I sit in my comfortable workroom where carpet is unstained, unstainable, and unremarkable. I look at it and remember wool rugs of a farm house. The rugs carried stains as coherent as a textbook: the darkness of blood when a younger cousin lost a finger in the pulley of a pump; a light space from spilled bleach; or unfaded bright spots beneath chairs—the signs of living, or (as the poet says) "all the appurtenances of home." I type on an old, old typewriter that was made in the '30s. At least that much respect can be shown the story.

When the tinker's wagon appeared on the road it caused a temporary stop in the work. That August when the trouble arose was as tricky as all Augusts. In August the last cut of hay comes in. Farmers gauge the weather sign, cut quickly, watch the horizon for storm as the hay dries. The baler comes through, the men following the tractor and wagon. They buck the bales. In the August when I was nine, the tinker appeared along the dusty road. I was too small to buck hay, was thus driving the tractor.

"Jim," my father said to me, "get the hell up to the house." He stood beside the wagon, shirt sodden with sweat, and sweat darkening the band of his straw hat. My father was a big man with English-blue eyes. He could be kind when he was unworried, but, what with the depression, he had not been unworried for years. My uncle and a cousin stood beside him. My uncle was from my mother's side. He was German, with eyes a thinner blue, and face a little starchy. Another cousin, my eldest, perched on top of the wagon where he stacked bales.

"I'd of thought," my uncle said about the tinker, "that the

bastard would have hit jail by now. Or made a little stop out there at the cemetery."

"Bullshit," my eldest cousin said from the top of the load. "He's working. He ain't a tramp." This was a cousin from dad's side. He was known for a smart mouth and radical notions.

"Bullshit back at you," my other cousin said. "Best you can say about him is that he might be a dago." This was a cousin from mom's side, and he was defending his father, who didn't need it.

I climbed from the tractor and headed across twenty acres to the house.

In the days before World War II a boy of nine was not a man, but he was treated as if he soon would be. He had responsibilities, and most boys that age took themselves seriously. If the tinker suddenly decided to rape and pillage there was not a whole lot I could do. That, however, was not the point. The point was that I represented a male presence.

Manhood comes in peculiar ways depending on where you grow. I recall walking across that field of hay stubble in bare feet. No town kid could have done it, although in the small towns boys shed their shoes with the last frost. By August their feet were as tough as mine. The difference was that they had no feel for the land. They did not know that land is supposed to hurt you a little. Weather the same. A farm is real, not pastoral.

An apparition stood at the edge of that twenty-acre hay field. Even today you occasionally see them in the midwest. Solitary black walnuts stand like intricately carved windmills. They spread against the sky, trees spared when the land was cleared. They grow slowly, and spare themselves. No other tree can root within their drip lines. Black walnuts spread poison through the soil.

This tree was a youngster when men and their families forged through the Cumberland Gap, or spread along rivers from a back-woods settlement called Chicago. Now it had a bole thirty feet in circumference. The first branches began at forty feet, and the total height was over a hundred. It ruled the fields, too majestic for human use. It would not serve for a children's swing, or for a hanging tree. Before first snow, when the guns came out for hunting season, we always gathered walnuts beneath spectral branches.

The tinker's wagon pulled into the lane as I passed the back door of the house. My grandmother saw me, looked toward the hayfield, and murmured to herself; probably a verse from Isaiah. At age nine I had small appreciation of women, did not understand that my grandmother was the most beautiful woman I would ever know. She was a storyteller, and she was tall in a time when most women were not. Her white hair fell below her waist when she brushed it. During the day she had it 'done up'. Her worn house-dresses were always pressed by flatirons. Her dresses fell to the tops of her shoes. My grandmother had been a young wife on the Oklahoma frontier when Indians roamed. The depression of the 1880s brought her back to Indiana.

The tinker's horses were wide from summer's roadside grass. One was bay, the other black. Color radiated from the wagon, red, white, and blue paint, green canvas, sun leaping from polished pans which clanked at every jolt in the rutted lane. Sun sparkled and danced against colors. My mother stepped from the house, my least cousin beside her, a girl of fifteen.

Did I understand what was going on? I doubt it, although I surely felt the men's displeasure and the women's pleasure. For my own part, the tinker's visit was exciting. Days on the farm are long. We had a telephone party line, but we had neither radio nor electricity. Townfolk had both.

It was a shy welcome the tinker faced, although he was accustomed to it. Since he moved from farm to farm, he met such welcomes all the time. Families learned how to comfortably handle each other. They had little experience with strangers.

"Missus," the tinker said to my grandmother, "I think of you last night and turn the horses this-a-way." His smile was a generalization among the sun-flashing pans, but he tipped his hat exactly toward my grandmother. His face was dark from either summer or blood. His brown eyes might have been those of a young Mediterranean girl. His eyes held no guile, and his face was—no more, no less—permanently relaxed and happy. In memory he seems a man without needs, an enlightened monk.

Even before he climbed from the wagon my least cousin passed him a dipper of water. Her young breasts moved beneath her housedress, her bobbed hair (which scandalized my grandmother) shone almost golden in sunlight. She had a pretty but puckish face, and lips that sometimes tied themselves with confusion. Although I had little appreciation of women, I was fascinated with what was happening to my cousin. Her body seemed to change every day. No doubt she was self-conscious as she became a woman, but to me she moved with confusing mystery.

"There's marriages all over," the tinker said. "From here to the county line." He drank, then climbed from the wagon. His horses stood placid as a puddle. The tinker not only repaired things, he also served as the county's newspaper. "The Baptists over in Warren bought a bell for the church. You can never tell what a Baptist is going to do." He said this last with a sort of wonder, but with no malice. He passed the dipper back to my least cousin and thanked her.

In the hayfield the men reached the end of a row. The tractor turned, headed back toward the house. I recall noting that another row would make a wagon load. The men would bring the load to the barn. Leaves of the black walnut looked ragged this late in August. The leaves carried no dust because the tree stood tall.

"It sounds like a busy winter," my mother said, and smiled at my least cousin.

"She was raised better," my grandmother said about my mother.

I had not the least notion what was meant. Now, of course, I understand that my mother spoke of the marriages.

"If this isn't the prettiest place on earth, then the Lord is fooling me." The tinker looked across fields toward the hardwood grove. Beyond the grove the river wound among rushes. At this time of year the river ran nearly clear. In spring, or after August storms, it ran brown with rich mud. The tinker looked toward our small farmhouse, then toward the barn. There was no hunger in his eyes, only happiness. He busied himself at repairing dreams.

The Great Depression, in spite of the softening that comes

with years, was gray. We were an ambitious people, but ambitions were set aside as we struggled against hard times. Grayness arrived because hard times did not end. Women lost color and men lost creative fire.

The tinker owned only his wagon and team, yet he magically wished for nothing. Because of this he allowed us to see our lives with new eyes. That was at least part of his magic. He did not want what we had, but he showed *us* how to want it. Looking back, I almost understand the other part of his magic.

"There's so much time for thinking," he said to my grandmother. "I wonder after your quilt while I drive." Copper-bottomed pans reflected sun, and the wagon seemed alight with the warmth of mighty candles. The black walnut stood indifferent as a tower. In mid-afternoon it threw a shadow shorter than itself. "Quilts take such a fine hand." The tinker did not say that he also had a fine hand.

"Margaret is growing up," my grandmother said about my least cousin. "She helps. Some day she'll be teaching me."

"She has a delicate way. That's a sign."

My cousin, strong enough to help with the heavy work of slaughtering, looked at her feet and blushed. In the everyday life of the farm my least cousin was no more delicate than a post, but that is not what the tinker meant. "Times are changing, but a lady will always show herself a lady." He turned to my mother, who had just made that unladylike and licentious comment about marriages. "She is also musical?" he asked about my least cousin. At the turn of the century farms had gained a few luxuries. Many farmhouses had pianos, but in the whole county only my mother excelled at music. She had a warm touch better suited for blues than for church. However, in those days we knew nothing about the musical blues.

"It takes a while to learn," my mother said. She did not say that my cousin took little interest. My mother actually blushed. Somehow she had been taken back into the fold of respectability, and the *how* of the matter seemed beyond explanation.

"There's so much to learn," the tinker said to my cousin.

"Takes a year, anyway, to rightly do a quilt."

Looking back, I understand that the tinker's magic truly was magic. At least it was magic in any terms we knew then, and certainly in any terms since.

I recall standing there, my bare feet as hard-soled as soil and callus could make them. I recall feeling that mysterious matters lived around me. The values of a farm are stern. I understood clean fence rows and upright dealing. I had been shown no other values. The word 'grace' had never entered my thought beyond its use in sermons.

The tinker's magic was to restore mystery and value to farm-women. No small undertaking.

Imagine a Depression farm. People lived close. A tyranny of custom was our only defense against wide knowledge of each other. When we dressed beside the kitchen woodstove on cold mornings the women dressed first. Then the men entered and dressed while the women went to the parlor. In unheated bed-rooms temperatures might fall below zero.

It takes time and privacy to be a lady. The farm offers only hog butchering, kitchen gardens, interminable days of canning, the tedious daily round of cooking and splitting wood and cleaning poultry sheds. Men's work is brutally hard. Women's work begins before dawn and ends with a nightly reading from the Bible.

"I saved back some mending," my grandmother said. "It's only a little."

In those days pots and pans were continually pushed from the hot to the cool side of the stove. Pans wore thin through years. We did not throw away a leaky pan.

I watched the tinker apply the patch, while from the barn came sounds of work as the men began to unload hay. The three women surrounded the tinker. The tinker drilled a clean hole through the leak, snapped on the pan patch, and worked to flatten it on an upright anvil. Deft fingers smoothed that patch into the pan with the skill of a carpenter using a finely-set plane. As he worked he spoke about a book of pictures from California. He tsked, then smiled. He mended a boot, and told about a new preacher. The preacher's wife was winning over the congregation, not the preacher. My memory calls back sunlight and quiet, above all, courtesy—an old-fashioned word.

"The sewing machine needs tinkering," my cousin said.

"I'll be but a minute," the tinker told his horses. He followed the three women toward the house. The horses stood almost as solidly as the black walnut. Shade spread dark beneath the wagon. My mother's shoulders did not slump as she walked. My grandmother, always busy, now seemed to stroll. My least cousin, clumsy with her growing up, was lithe in her movement. My heart pounded like rifle shots. I stood knowing I should follow, yet was somehow daunted. Even at age nine I understood that privacy lived in this encounter. A loud curse came from the barn. I looked to see my German cousin leap from the hay wagon and stride toward me.

"Are you ever going to grow up, Jimmy boy?" My cousin passed me, not running, but striding. Over by the barn the other men hesitated, then decided my cousin could handle matters. They returned to work, could not admit the work was hopeless.

Jaws of depression gnawed. No matter how hard men struggled, failure and despair were triumphant. Some years we did not make seed money. The bill for land tax stood dark as that black tree.

The sewing machine sat in a corner of the invaded parlor, and the tinker knelt. He removed a worn sleeve from the treadle. He spoke of a neighbor's daughter, studying at Ball State Teacher's College.

My cousin stood in the doorway. I stood behind him, embarrassed to be there, unable to not be there. The three women watched the tinker. My mother laughed. My grandmother said that college would be good for that particular girl. My least cousin yearned after the tinker's words. To us, college was a grand and remote place. I fidgeted. My grandmother turned, saw us in the doorway.

"Ralph," she said to my cousin, "this is not your place."

I do not know how scorn and sadness can combine in such a

low voice. The tinker knelt above his work, but for a moment he fumbled with his wrench. My mother turned. I had never seen such anger from my mother, never saw such anger afterwards. My least cousin blushed and stood silent. The man in the doorway stiffened. He stood rigid as a rifle.

"You'd take away what little joy there is," my grandmother said. "Get about your business." She turned back. My mother looked at me, and I did not understand her quick sadness. Nor, probably, did she.

I sat in the kitchen with Ralph as the tinker finished his work. The man sat with fists closed. His blue eyes turned pale as his face. He fought shame with anger, and while his eyes remained pale his face gradually heated. "We'll see," he kept muttering. "We'll see about this."

That night—with the tinker long departed—marked the crossroads of my growing up. A curious silence lived in kitchen and parlor. We were isolated hearts. My mother avoided speaking with my father. My grandmother murmured to my least cousin, had nothing to say to the men. My least cousin worked in complete silence. Darkness lay across the fields by eight o'clock. Exhausted and sullen men made thin excuses to get out of the house, then made no excuse. They piled in the Ford and left on the road to town. For the first time in memory, I went to bed without hearing my father read a passage from the Bible.

No one spoke because no one knew what to say. A stranger came among us. He wielded the power of appreciation, and the power of unneeding affection.

Night passed. Morning arrived with sullen silence. Haying continued, although on that day the men were dragged-out. We made slow progress. When we went to the house for dinner at noon, the women spoke indifferently. An awful resignation dwelt among the women, a permanent tiredness of spirit. I never again remember spontaneity in that house.

The telephone party line buzzed with news. The tinker's wagon had burned. The tinker was intact. His horses had been un-hitched and tied. They were also intact, but the wagon of red and white and blue and green was in ruins. . . .

I wish this story could end here. I would be compelled by its darkness, would feel such sorrow, but would not have to feel the rest. I sit in my comfortable workroom and type on this antique machine that was new when the world went spoiled. The tinker was not a man who would seek revenge. Perhaps he taught what old mystics knew, that wisdom arrives on the breath of inexplicable pain.

We got the hay in, and we had three days of storm. Sunday came with church and Sunday School. Cornfields stood bright, dust gone from leaves washed beneath August thunder. The land expressed grain, but lives turned dull as sermons. We left church and drove the graveled road which lay like a glowing path, but our way led back to the farm.

We were met by sparkles of light dancing among the tattered leaves of that spectral walnut. My mother gasped, remained silent. My grandmother chuckled. My least cousin was so confused she seemed about to weep.

"Get to the house," my uncle said to the women. "I don't want to hear a word." He climbed from the car and stood staring at the walnut. "How in the hell did he do it?"

The tree was alight with polished pans. They hung far out on branches. Pans glowed silver and copper, iron and enamel. No one could climb that tree. Even if a man could, it would be impossible to inch far enough out on the branches.

"He must have nailed boards like steps, then took 'em back down," my English cousin said. "He must of used a pole and hooked that stuff out there. The man is slick." My English cousin, known for radical notions, was not about to defect from us. At the same time he could appreciate what he saw.

"Jim," my father said, "go get the goddamn rifle."

In a sense it was I who defected. Over the next two years I grew closer to my mother and grandmother. My least cousin turned seventeen. She married. The men became silent and critical, but we still worked. Trapped in questions, I became silent. We avoided our confusions.

At the end of two years we lost the farm to taxes. The world started talking about war, but even that most hideous of wars leaves no memory this enduring:

The tinker used piano wire. Bullets only glanced, causing the pans to dance. We shot at the handles, broke a few pans loose. Work called and we worked. The crops came in.

We fired, and fired, and fired; pings, rattles, the sound of bullets. Autumn departed into winter, and shotguns cleared the walnuts. We spoke of cutting the tree, but did not. We fired as new leaves budded in the spring. Guns tore away small branches, and until we lost the farm they tore at my understanding.

My uncle was tight-lipped when we left the farm. My father wept, but my mother did not. I remember the tractor standing silent in the fields, and a few straggling pans hanging in the walnut. I remember our farm truck loaded with household furnishings, and wish that this were all. It is not, however; for what I remember always, can never forget, are two years of wasted ammunition and the sounds of firing, the silhouettes of raised weapons, the rattle of bullets as men sought redemption; through all the seasons shooting guns into that tree.

THE PATRIARCH

□ □ □

THE PATRIARCH

"A HILL TOO STEEP FOR SLEDDING." SOL SAID THAT TWO days before he died. "God is a character, but picky where He puts His hills."

"If you are ten years old," I said, "it is a wonderful hill." I knew what he was going to next say about God. I just wanted to hear him say it.

"A hill to keep old men alive," Sol said. "Puts sparkle in the toes." He inched up the hill, and he looked at the surrounding brick buildings which had been standing for about as long as we had; which in Sol's case was seventy years, and in my own case seventy-three. The sunlight over Seattle seemed to flatten the red brick, and it glazed the dusty windows of the mostly abandoned buildings. My old man's feet were comfortably sweaty, for at this age sweat is a luxury.

"So being picky, He wouldn't waste a good sled hill in such a country," Sol said. "This place has no snow. Remember, this is the rabbi telling you."

I have often wished that I were a Jew. No matter how old they are, or where they are, Jews have fathers.

In mixed sunlight and shadow, in Seattle, we were spending our last day together. We both knew it, and we were giving thanks for such a day. At our backs Puget Sound lay like a blue pond, and the distant mountain range was still peaked with snow. The spring melt had not reached above seven thousand feet. It was a day to be born on, to be married on. It was a day for old men to walk in the sun. It was a day for falling in love, for sailing to India; a day for buying flowers—spice—tea—silks—a day for giving flowers—

tea—silks; like old-time suitors beckoning to wives of many years. A gift of a day, a day of gifts. A Victorian day, complete with the lace of sunlight.

"The belly," Sol said. "Think about it." He took a step that covered eight inches, then rested on his walking stick. He seemed to hover over the stick, an enormous man, but fading now. His hands were smooth, pale, and his nose was a slab, his graying eyebrows like bushes sprouting on rocky ground. His face was also pale.

"Your belly?"

"Mine will do," he said, "since it gets the operation."

"I worry about Benjy," I told him. "Jerome can maybe handle this. Sam can maybe handle this." I was naming his three sons. Benjy is the youngest, and Benjy is forty-two. "Can Sarah handle this?" Sarah is his wife.

"God is a trickster," Sol told me. "He gives me a Presbyterian belly. Don't tell me about Sarah."

"Still, I worry."

"You have better things to do," Sol said. "I'll worry for you. Quit worrying. It infarcts the belly." In the street, between the old buildings, and weaving casually uphill with its lights blinking slowly like the driver had forgotten to shut them off, an ambulance headed for the hospital at the top of the hill. We were headed for that same hospital. The ambulance stopped at a traffic light. When the light changed it rolled backward for a short distance before surging forward. A whole line of traffic rolled backward, then surged forward.

"The heart," Sol said, "is a Jew. The mouth, the tongue, all Yiddish." He stepped another eight inches. "They have all the fun. Think of the fatted calves, the wine, the loaves of bread, the cheeses. Seventy years across the tongue, down the gullet, to feed a Presbyterian."

"The rabbi is telling me."

"Because," he explained, "the belly has no fun. The heart and tongue have fun. The poor belly does the slave work. A sweat shop beneath this buckle." He patted his waist. There was no buckle. He could no longer wear a belt. His gut was swollen.

When we were younger, when we were fifty and forty-seven and first met, Sol was muscular and quick; at least quick for a rabbi. I, Louis Pegourie, was also muscular, but quicker. My quickness came from an early life spent in logging with my father's crews in Canada. When my father was killed in a logging accident, I became a reader of books. Most likely because the books held sense, and the accident was senseless. When Sol and I met, I worked at the public library. The rabbi and the reader. Twenty years. Not a long time after all. Once a month in those years, or at least once every six weeks, we had managed to spend an afternoon together. "Because," Sol had once told me, "I get tired of only the Jews. You are a nonsectarian friend of books. You are greatly, wonderfully irreligious."

"Not irreverent," I recall saying.

"What am I telling you? Was I making words about reverence?"

It is supposed to be terribly hard to be old. I don't find it so. It is hard to be sick, to be sometimes weak. The worst part is that the world treats you as if you were stupid. This man beside me, for instance, had written a larger number of books than many people have read. I have done my share as well. Yet the world hollers at you and ignores you; and that is what is wrong with being old. The hills grow steeper, yes, but old men still walk those hills. Young men do not have the time. We stepped forward, and I wondered how a concrete sidewalk could be laid on such a steep hill. Surely the wet concrete would run downhill before it set. What is hard about being old is that there is less time to learn, and to think about what you learn.

"Sarah," Sol said, and stepped further up the hill. "1934. New York. Depression."

"I was twenty-three."

"I was twenty, but she was seventeen," Sol said. "Her father was a practical man. All starch. I won a bet." Beside us a street tree was just coming into leaf. It was only a little stick of a tree, and to protect it the street department had placed an iron grate around it. The grate stood like a little fence. Sol tapped the grate with his stick. "No consideration for dogs," he said. "Suppose you are a poodle with a bladder that feels like a Great Dane. Suppose you come along here, your eyes swimming with pee, and they've put up this grate."

"You'd pee."

"But think of the compromise. A world without honor." He turned to look back down the hill. "We are progressing," he said, "and I am in no hurry." Out on Puget Sound the sea traffic was heavy. A blue and white Alaska ferry looked like it was shaving the bows of an outgoing tanker, although of course it was not. A small Navy craft, maybe a minelayer, was a black dot beside the larger ships. A hundred or more sailboats were like snowflakes on the water.

"Her father did not want her engaged to a scholar. The Great Depression. Even practical men could not get jobs. So who needs a scholar?"

"You bet with him? Practical men don't bet. I have it first hand from Montaigne. I have it first hand from Thoreau."

"Montaigne," Sol said. "I have my doubts. What does a French politician know, him and his phony tower?" He turned back up the hill. "I bet myself," he said, "that I could get a job. If I lost, I lost her." He tapped the sidewalk twice with his stick. "Romance. Of course, I was younger then." He stepped upward a bit more strongly. "Among the Jews," he said, "a father is no joke." His belly was hurting him. If you know a man long enough, you learn to read most of the different ways in which he smiles. "Still," he said, "I made a joke. I went to her uncle, her father's brother, and borrowed ten dollars. . . ." We were near the corner where the ambulance had stopped. Traffic lined up behind a stop light.

"The first stop lights in New York," he said, "were installed in 1928. They had a bronze statue on top of each one. Before that the police directed traffic . . . of course, that has nothing to do with the joke. With the ten dollars I bought a job from a man who was selling jobs. 'Can you cut flank steak,' he says. I say, do you want the ten dollars? He says, 'report for work' and sent me to a restaurant.

On the way I stop at my aunt's flat because my aunt has the brains of the family. She—one—two—three—teaches me how to slice any kind of meat. I mean, here, even, pig's knuckles." He watched the traffic light. "We have to get across this side street," he said. He stared at the sky, and deadpanned. "A little shove there, God. Let's have a little shove."

He was starting to make me angry. Sol always could do that.

"Don't die," I said. "Such a humorist. Such a loss to the world." He did not answer right away. We were busy crossing the street. It was a narrow street, but the crossing was all uphill.

"In two years I was head cook," he told me. "Don't worry about Sarah. Sarah has sons. This business about Sarah. Do you think the Book of Ruth is a joke?"

"You are the humorist."

"The joke was," Sol said, "that Sarah's uncle had to borrow the ten dollars from Sarah's father." We stood on the corner, not yet ready to tackle the last long block. That next block was the steepest part of the hill. My legs hurt, especially the one that had been broken once when working in the woods. Still, if he could haul that belly I could haul a couple of hurting legs.

"I courted," Sol said. "Ah. Oh. I bought flowers at a second-hand flower shop on 34th. I swore to myself that someday she would have a house and I would raise flowers for her. To this day I don't really know how much she likes flowers." He looked into the street. "Uh, oh, poor Benjamin. The fix is in."

A large, new car pulled into the sidestreet and stopped. It parked illegally, and Sol's son Benjy climbed out. Benjy is big, like his father, and he wears expensive dark suits, dark like his shiny car, silk ties, a diamond ring. He walked toward us looking for all the world like a little boy trapped in grown-up clothes.

"Papa," he said. "Hello, Louis," he said.

Sol leaned on his stick. Waited. Benjy was actually blushing. "Your brothers sent you," Sol asked, and his voice was kind.

"They are waiting at the hospital. They are worried because you are late." Benjy's voice was a whisper of embarrassment.

"The hospital has been waiting for seventy years," Sol said, and his voice was still kind. "You go along now, Benjy, and we'll be there soon enough."

"Papa, I can give you a ride."

"This is your father speaking."

"Yes, papa."

"But later, you will drive Louis home."

Benjy, a big man, Benjy, and yet he walked back to his car and did not look big at all. He was too embarrassed. Sol turned, to look up the last long grade. "This is getting serious," he said. "I expected that it would." He looked across the street at an abandoned house. "They had fine workers in brick around this city. A pity for the buildings. So misused." The second floor of the house still had windows. The sun lay like golden satin across the dusty windows.

"So it's serious," he said. "All right my friend, we proceed." He stepped upward a short pace, and then another short pace. "We go to rejoin the Jews."

"We are meeting your family."

"Don't be fooled. Before this is through, half of my last congregation will come through that hospital." He looked further up the hill, where the hospital rose tall and white in the sun. "Temple builders," he said. "Physicians need temples. It makes them secure about their balls."

"Why are you doing this?" It was a fair question. The man was dying. The operation would simply kill him a bit sooner.

"The family has hope. The family believes in miracles." His face was even paler, if that was possible. "Miracles. Strange." He rested on his stick, then turned once more to watch the water and the mountains. Dark patches lay here and there across the water, shaded patches from high and scattered clouds. He turned back, upward.

"My first congregation met in a store front. Then the store front was torn down. We met in the storeroom of another store, like old-time Quakers in living rooms. A long time ago. Now there are babies in my last congregation, who I don't even know their names. Babies. It continues, but the congregation is too large. It needs to split and regroup. Hah. Try telling them that."

We stepped for awhile in silence. I wished that we could weep together, but Sol was not the weeping type. We were both too old to rail against this, and death itself is only one more adventure. Death is no problem, but dying is frightening. I thought of my first wife, Jenny, who died in childbirth. I have no sons, no daughters.

"My friend," he said when we were halfway up the block, "do not be fooled. I am no Moses. For more than forty years I have led my people, but Moses was denied. I have never been denied. The rabbi is luckier than Moses."

"You have a fine family. You have a fine reputation. Sol, it is all deserved."

"I also have the Jews," he said, "and that is important. And yes, maybe I deserve it, maybe not, but I will not complain against it. Meanwhile, I have a burden for you."

"What do you need? What can I give?"

"My family," he said. "I know them. When I am gone they will require something from you."

"Whatever I can do."

"Remember that," he said. "Do what you *can* do. Do not try to do what you cannot."

When we arrived at the hospital, ascending the last of the hill and walking across a courtyard of white stone, his family did not come flocking into the courtyard, the sons, the wives of sons. They managed to restrain themselves and allow him that final courtesy. Sarah met him at the door. He turned back to me. He embraced me, kissed my cheek. "Go with God," he said. "Benjy will drive you home."

When Benjy dropped me off I went to my room, and stayed waiting for the inevitable phone call. I read from work of St. John Of The Cross, and a detective novel. In two days Sol was dead, a quiet death under anesthetic. That was the only bad part, for knowing Sol, he would have been so interested in dying. I regretted for him that he had not been awake. At the same time, I was occupied with my own grief. For two more days I remained in my room, confused and sometimes weeping. I thought of my second wife, and the loss did not seem less with the years. I remembered Sol's kiss, his blessing. Then, on a spring evening, I walked a block down the hill to the Chinese store where they know me. I bought two candles, special ones that were not on the store's shelves. Religion is a joke, but St. Therese and St. Jude are not jokes.

The spring seemed to drag. It did not have the explosions of flowers that have attended other springs. The flowers bloomed, but nature itself seemed reluctant. Benjy came to visit twice that spring. He did not know what he wanted. Talking to him, it was clear that the family was not doing well. It handled its grief, but it was huddling together. Fearful. Some amorphous force seemed to be attempting to spread the family, disperse it. I could see the problem, could give no help. Sol had been so strong, that the family no longer felt the force of strength in their world. Benjy was having a terribly hard time, and his formal mourning did not seem to be helping much. A ritual that was not working.

I mostly spent the days walking in the sun. The nights were difficult. Memories. I have lost everyone, except for Sol's family. In the nights I thought of my lost wives. I have had good luck with women, but the women had no luck. My first wife was Jenny. We were married in our early twenties. We had seven happy, kid-crazy years together. She died in childbirth. The child died. I did not touch another woman until I was fifty, because of fear. Then I married Margaret, who was my same age, and who worked beside me at the library. We had thirteen quiet years, and I woke one morning to find her dead beside me. Stroke. I wanted to die and could not. Life insists. Interminably. There is no honor in suicide. Sometimes at night I recalled the burden Sol had given me. I wondered what that service was which must yet be performed.

Benjy is a fine man. Of Sol's sons, perhaps Benjy is the best. He is sensitive. When he finally came to me, in June, he was not phony. He was not lying.

"My mother is dying," he said. "I do not think I can bear this." He sat, all fine suit and tie, in my old room. He did not see the faded wallpaper, the smoky ceilings. He only saw me. "She is in the hospital," he said. "Louis, please come with me."

Naomi. The Book of Ruth. Maybe Sarah was dying, but I had my doubts. Sarah had sons, and those sons had just lost a father. Those sons had not yet gotten hold of their individual strengths. Dying, to Sarah, was out of the question, no matter how ill. However, there was no possible way to explain that to Benjy.

"You go to the hospital," I told him, "and I will be along directly." I live on the hill, not a good place for an old man, but it is near the library. When Benjy left I walked the hill to the hospital, as a testament to Sol. A trellis of roses stood behind a fence. I reached through the fence, picked two.

Sarah is a small woman. Tough. As tough as her sons would be someday. Outside her room, one of her daughters-in-law, Hannah, waited, and supervised some of the grandchildren who clustered in the waiting room or drifted up and down the hallway. Boys and girls, some of them nearly young men and women. Soon there would be great-grandchildren.

"Louis," Hannah said, "there is more trouble inside that room than you can see at first. Everyone is nearly out of control." Hannah is tall, fair-haired, and a woman to trust. A high school teacher. If a high school teacher says a situation is out of control, it pays to listen.

"Sam," I asked. Sam is the oldest son. He should be leading.

"He is trying," she told me. "He is trying so hard that he just adds to the problem."

The men were there, the women, and three of the oldest grandchildren. Sarah's bed was raised so that she was nearly sitting. When I entered there was silence, and it was pretty clear that there had been little but silence. That is no way to run an illness.

"So, Sarah," I said, "is this a joke you are making?"

She smiled. It was as if she had not smiled for a long time and was pleased because she remembered how. Her hair, nearly all gray, is getting a little thin. Her small mouth is still firm, and the smile seemed girlish. She reached to touch my hand. "Louis," she said, "a few tests, a little flushing of the system. Tell these people."

"Wailing walls are in bad taste," I said to whoever was listening, and they all were. "This is a matter of taste. You want to remember that." I looked at them. Benjy, troubled, fear in his eyes. Sam, nearly sullen from his responsibility. Jerome, a little too eager, like a man who wants to do something, anything, to help; a man to set in motion, if a direction could be discovered. The wives, Grace and Janet, the children, Jacob and Clara and Sally; the children, confused.

"Look at them," I said to Sarah. "They look like a Mormon choir. That Joseph Smith might have lived to see this. So many Jewish converts."

There was a stirring in the room. Something half felt. Like the stirring of faint hope. Jerome took a deep breath. He looked like he was about to charge back and forth, back and forth, in help or celebration. Jerome is the lean, wiry one of Sol's sons. He is quick. He is fast in reading a situation.

They needed something, and they sensed that they were about to find it. They had been so fearful, so confused, that they had not even known what they needed. They needed to know that force and strength still lived.

"My friend the rabbi," I said, "if he were here, would make a joke. Joseph Smith would run. Humorless, these Mormons." I raised my right hand, but slowly. Sarah took my left hand. Her small hand was anything but frail. She pressed my hand, a kind of confidence and reassurance; and I needed it, because it was going to take nerve and luck to pull this off. Jerome stepped to the doorway, whispered, and Hannah entered the room. The children stood, nearly afraid. My right hand floated in the air, untrembling; an old man's hand, but it did not tremble.

"Benjamin," I said. "Here beside me." He stepped forward, confused but glad. I lowered my hand, kissed him, took his hand. Sarah released my left hand.

No, Sol had not been Moses, but he had led his people. He had led these people, and when he died he had the Jews. Sol was lucky. Golden lucky.

I began to speak, and I lowered my left hand, pressing it gently against Sarah's cool forehead. The words, the old, old words, came so easily. My voice did not tremble. I felt the union,

the community, the family return to itself; as steadily, ageless,
I gave my reverent, patriarchal blessing.

THE CURIOUS CANDY STORE

□   □   □

THE CURIOUS CANDY STORE

CITIES ARE NOT SUPPOSED TO HAVE ALCOVES, BUT PLACID City does. The Curious Candy Store still stands two blocks from our old grade school, and the school itself stands in what amounts to an alcove. When any of us return we feel that we step across time. Traffic buzzes everywhere, until we cross the center line of Maple Street and our feet find the inner curb.

In this place it might as well be 1930, or 1910. Victorian houses stand newly painted. Outside one house a bronze deer ornaments a huge lawn behind wrought iron fences. Summer breezes lay light fingers on mown grass, and the breezes touch ornamental stained glass windows as if everything here were kissing cousins.

At the Curious Candy Store the old woman who always ran the place stands still behind the counter. By anybody's reckoning, she must be a hundred and thirty years old by now. That isn't right, but unless time itself is playing games we know it's the truth.

Children still enter, and they emerge with licorice whips, jawbreakers, lemon drops, stick candy, and occasionally a balloon. I remember the magic of childhood, and remotely recall the day I left the candy store with my own balloon. The balloon was red and bouncy in a breeze that danced fancy figures around the grade school. The day was filled with autumn light.

A red balloon. No child was ever given more than one, and for reasons we did not understand red was a little scary. Green was good, and blue might be, sometimes. I think we feared—even if we did not look over our shoulders—the yellow ones and the white ones. We were hopeful with orange. Who, after all, remembers their fears at age six? Older and tougher kids on the playground always yelled about gray and black balloons, but in our day no one ever saw one.

But those days of my childhood, before World War II, were not so complicated as days are now. It was still easy to recognize magic during the long summers and autumns. Many families did not even have radios, and televisions were unknown. Since it was the time of the Great Depression children had few toys. We played 'make believe'. So much of our play came from our own imaginations that it was no surprise if a balloon talked to you in a tinkling voice.

"Dum hiddly dee-dum, play as you grow. Red is so chancy, it's scary, you know?"

I am an old man now, visiting an old neighborhood, and watching children pass. The Curious Candy Store sells bubble gum and baseball cards and malted milk balls.

"It's color, it's color, it's color, you see. Play always with color, oh hum diddle dee."

Most of the balloons popped, of course. A few of them got loose and went tumbling into blue sky. Even fewer made it to home or school, where they either burst or slowly deflated.

I grew and became an artist, never an easy task. Color and light and depth ran through my dreams. There were years and years of struggle, and yes, the color red is chancy. Color itself—or rather playing with color—can lead you through divorces and booze and decades of rejection. At the end lies great success, but one travels a badly cobbled road.

Some led vanilla lives, those who received the white balloons. They grew and married and loved and worked and had children. Nothing really bad ever happened to them, and perhaps they were luckiest of all. Blue was considered good, sometimes, and blue balloons slipped from the fingers of future teachers and politicians. Green showed the way to actors and gardeners. Orange produced musicians, businessmen, interior decorators. We all grew and left the neighborhood, but some return.

I think time freezes in a few small places around the globe.

There's nothing cosmic about it, and there's no grand scheme. In spite of what our scientists say, time has a way of doing what it wants.

Sometimes it wants to be fey. This is surely the way that time hoards up memories. Maybe in Egypt, somewhere, scholars still write on scrolls. Perhaps in China one small section of the Great Wall stands newer than new.

And so this neighborhood is a place where time collects memories. The balloons contained our futures. I know that now, because of all the things that have happened. Rather, the balloons carried the spirits of who we might become. A lot depended on us.

However, there is more to it than that. The old woman at the Curious Candy Store still gives balloons. Children pass with grave faces and grave eyes.

When I entered the store after fifty years away, it seemed smaller. The oak counter was the same, and the gleaming candy jars still stood ranked like soldiers. Kites and kite string were arranged in bins. Party favors and tin whistles, and the little tin crickets, lay in careful arrangement on shelves. Pink and blue packages of birthday candles were stacked beside crepe paper streamers of gold and silver. The ceiling was lower than I remembered, and soft sheens of polished oak and glowing glass stirred childish memories. I felt yearning, and a kind of dazzlement before the sight and smells of candy fish and peppermints.

Only one thing had changed. There were different candies. Of course, these are different times, and I suppose children are never horrified by candy. There were other things. What I took to be baseball cards were cards of a different kind, men with red staining their beards. Comic books were different, which surely meant that childhood was different.

"Go away," the old woman said, as she squinted in dim light and finally seemed to recognize me. "You can't come back here. Why would you want to?"

She looked the same. Her white hair was bound in a gypsy scarf, and her long dress was faded purple with carefully ironed pleats. Eyes, brown as the chocolate she sold, were not unkind, only factual. Her hands were nimble, and her face was webbed in wrinkles.

"You were old when my father was a child," I said in bewilderment. I felt in the presence of mystery, but maybe the mystery could be solved. "Is there some eternal game you are forced to play?" I asked. "Are you trapped here?" Kindness and concern brought layers of gentleness to my voice.

"I will be here when your great-grandchildren are old," she said. Her voice was not angry, only sad. "You should not be here. You grew up and lost your childhood. Will you now insist on losing your childhood memories?"

"I only inquire."

"You inquire in the wrong place," she told me. "There's only one future to a customer, and you've had yours. Be content."

"There are changes here."

"I'm a merchant," she said. "I stock what sells." She turned away, dismissing me.

I should have left then. Only a fool would stay. "You are more than a merchant."

"You should leave," she said, "but since you have not . . ." She rubbed her forehead, just below the line drawn by the scarf. The woman was not unkind, only dispassionate. "I am time incarnate," she told me. "I *am* memory. You deal with powerful forces."

Memories of childhood surrounded me. Reminders of childhood lay on shelves; jump ropes and balsa model kits. I felt overwhelmed by the magic and play that are never far from a child's mind. I felt the hopes and fears of a child—small hopes and fears in adult memory, but they were not small at the time. The memories began to grow.

"You sell memories," I said, and pointed to some of the candy and cards. "These are not good memories."

"They are the best memories still in stock," she said curtly. "I didn't make the world, I only live in it."

Later, I would realize that her very curtness was a denial of memories. It denied gentle fingers of wind caressing grass, of my mother's voice calling me home from play as night fell. Of course, these days, even in this quiet neighborhood, children are no longer allowed to play outside in the gathering dusk.

"If you can work small miracles, if you can give away spirits of the future, I could hope the children would have better futures."

"I give the only futures that are available." She looked through the small front window onto the quiet street, the seemingly quiet neighborhood. "There are no simple futures now. Including what is left of yours." She paused, watching me, and she was neither kind nor unkind. "Although if you leave your own memories here, maybe I can turn them into some child's future."

I went away quickly. When you are old, memories are what you own.

But I did not leave quickly enough. These days I remember that I once had memories, and even what they were. A creaking swing on the front porch. A schoolmate practicing piano, and the notes of the piano on a warm evening breeze. I no longer remember how the memories felt. Hope is gone, as is excitement. Love has disappeared, and when I place paint to canvas no spirit rises from the work. It is only paint and canvas.

And so I sit, an old man, shuddering as I watch children pass. Their balloons carry colors unknown in my time: fluorescents of hot pink, hysteric pastels of beige and turquoise, and not a primary color in the lot.

There are gray balloons, and there are black. Black balloons dance in the breeze.

I wonder what the balloons are whispering, and feel the horror of those futures; the only feeling I have left. I watch because, maybe, fashioned from flimsy and from my own lost memories, perhaps a last brightly dancing balloon will pass.

BY REASON OF DARKNESS

□   □   □

BY REASON OF DARKNESS

Teach us what we shall say unto him; *for* we cannot
order *our speech* by reason of darkness.   —*Job* 37:19

NOW THE CORPSES ARE DECAYED, NOT INTO DUST, BUT
have become one with the fertile and well-watered soil of the val-
leys. Sun illuminates the forests, and pries into those dark places
where moss is gray and lighter green. Even the skeletons (one sup-
poses) have become soil, although no doubt a polished white fragment is occasionally washed from the hills; the bone glowing
spectral and jewel-like in a setting of foliage. Houses are rebuilt.
Rice paddies are tended. If ghosts walk that wet land—and, ghosts
always have—perhaps we who did so much killing there are still
remembered. The living try to forget.

We came in landing craft and aircraft, and we breathed the
hot screams of war. We left, as if blown by a cold exhalation. A
sigh, a murmur from the congregated dead.

You ask which war? It makes no difference. They are all the
same. Only the terrain differs sometimes. Every few years there is
an improvement in weapons. There is never an improvement in
illusions.

I was amazed to find I still had illusions when I received the
phone call from Bjorn North. He lived in a small town on the
Strait of Juan de Fuca in Washington State. He fished sometimes,
drank much of the time, and when the fishing was bad he ran
drugs in a small way.

"I called the Blackbird," he said. "Blackbird is coming. I want
you both here."

"The Blackbird is insane," I said. "He isn't just Asiatic, the
way we may be. The Bird is genuinely insane." There is a reason
for Bird's insanity, and we both knew it.

"This is more than a reunion," I said into the phone. "What do you want?"

"I have to make a judgment call," North said, "and only you and Blackbird will understand." North's voice cracked, whispered, lingered over syllables like a man hesitating as he fumbled in a foreign language. I could imagine him hunched inside a phone booth overlooking a harbor where clusters of masts stood shrouded in evening fog. The man was as tall as I am, but without the balding head and hook nose. It is a gray wet land in which he lived. His long legs would swell the seams of his pants at the shanks. His narrow chest would seem dubbed onto the body of a wrestler, and above it would ride his equally narrow and Scandinavian face, like a new moon with blond hair. He was a man who looked built in two parts; from waist down a football lineman, from waist up stretched like a swimmer.

"Are you drinking?" When he was drinking he had a bad habit of laughing—a white face turning red—a red mouth grotesque. Obscenity often amused him.

"Not enough," he said. "If you mean am I sober, the answer is I'm afraid to get drunk." The phone connection carried an echo, one muddled and faint.

"Stay sober. Stay dry for two days. It will take me that long to get there." I paused. North was not fundamentally a liar, although there has probably never been such a thing as a completely truthful sailor.

"What are you afraid of?" I asked.

His voice was a guarded whisper, like a man dredging a secret from the deep well of fright. "I'm afraid there is no safe place to die."

War is normal. If it were not, we would stop having so many of them. One problem with war is that the men who fight are generally voiceless. Even if they find their voices no one listens. No one can *afford* to listen. When the war is over the men who survive put on civilian clothes and disappear into the crowd. Occasionally one of them camps alongside a freeway with a rifle, or he tosses his girlfriend from a seven-story window, or he bunkers up and dies in a firefight with the police. Newspapers report the event. People shake their heads and say, "My, my," and "Good God." They are surprised, but the real surprise is not that a few do it, but that thousands do not.

A war produces corpses, but it does not bury them. At least it doesn't bury them deep. I suspected that North's corpses were coming back to greet him, for we all have a string of spirits trailing at our back. They are like the anchoring tail of an enormous kite. If you handle them with respect, they only whisper a little bit sometimes, and the trail behind you is faded and vague. Handle them wrong—as North was now finding out—and your corpses turn from mist to the dark smoke of napalm.

"Are you dying?"

"Not right away," he said, "at least not if I can help it."

"I will not help you kill yourself. I'm no longer tuned to it, even to help a friend." I nearly added, "Even when that friend is in such a state of fear."

He was shocked. Not because of what he heard, but because I spotted a weakness he tried to conceal.

"I want to live," he said. "If I need killing I'll ask the Blackbird."

It was then that I discovered I still had illusions. A friend was in need. Maybe it was possible to help. "Sit tight," I told him. "Forty-eight hours."

It was August, a droning time in my San Francisco law office. The place could run without me for a week. My secretary is a private person. She asked only essential questions. My secretary, Miss Molly, is a forty-five-year-old spinster in a day when spinsters are supposed to be extinct. She did not mean for it to be that way. Jews have close-knit families. I know, because I come from one. Miss Molly's mother died young. Molly was the youngest daughter. Her career was first housekeeper, now nurse, to her aged father.

"The Blackbird," she said. "It sounds like bad television."

"That's how it sounds," I told her. "The smart Jew lawyer, the Hunky fisherman, and the King Kong Negro. But for once you're wrong. The Bird is small. He even looks like a bird."

Albert Bird is so black that he seems pure African. He could kill Miss Molly while he was shaking her hand. She would be dead before the smile of greeting left her face. The Blackbird is not a highly trained killer. He simply has a talent.

"This is real," she said, as she packed a folder of legal work in my briefcase. "Just in case things get unreal."

The odds on my killing again seemed long. Not impossible. When I returned from war it was to discover that when men hate their lives, or cannot come to terms with them, they must fight against killing those who are familiar or loved. It took a long time to learn. My wife divorced me, largely, I think, because she feared the forces she sensed lying behind my tenderness. At any rate, wives are in danger, and secretaries. When the men do not understand what drives them, the wives and secretaries are in awful danger. Miss Molly is as rare as dinosaurs. It would be a crime to throw the last dinosaur from this thirty-story building.

Sometimes the men kill each other, and for those same reasons of love. But more of that later.

"I believe," she said, as I packed a pistol in the briefcase, "I'm supposed to remind you to save the last round for yourself." She was not being sarcastic, exactly. She was not being humorous, because she was not smiling. She is small, dark haired, unsmiling. A cynic, but not bitter.

I like her for her toughness. Miss Molly does not ask for sympathy, and does not give it in matters short of a death in the family. She knows what sort of monster she works beside. Maybe she thinks of *me* as the last dinosaur.

The route from San Francisco wound past the outskirts of Chinatown. Many-colored banners. Tourists. Shops selling imitation jade, bamboo, rice paper, tea, goldfish. All of it a façade, or maybe not. Opium. Sweatshops. Money. Smuggling of every commodity, especially illegal-immigrant Chinese. We fight war after war in the Orient. The Orient always wins. It absorbs, takes us over; we disappear into its enormous yawn.

Bad television? The Blackbird's insanity makes him unable to lie. It makes him consult with pigs, dogs, goldfinches; long conversations. He hears their voices. Insanity causes his celibacy. He fears children, or rather, he fears fathering them. Were a daughter or granddaughter to climb on his knee and ask what he did in the war, the Blackbird would say: "I killed little girls just like you. They got in the way."

But to Molly it can only seem like bad television. She does not know the Bird, although she knows some of the rest of us. The rest of us do not suffer the Blackbird's affliction. The rest of us know how to lie.

If my daughter asked what I did in the war the answer would be: "I sat in the CIC on a destroyer, eating donuts, and fired rockets." I would not tell her those rockets were fired at quadrants on a grid, a list of quadrants chosen by a computer programmed to probability of enemy movements. I would not tell her it was impossible to know what was in each quadrant—an enemy camp, a marketplace, a convent, a grade school. I would say nothing about those days in the jungle with North and the Blackbird.

San Francisco to Seattle is a hard day's drive if you take the freeways. I took the coast route which is interminably slow; a two-day drive. It was a matter of self-protection, a matter of preparation. The mind is not always so strong and exact as we like to believe. I was driving toward some dark hysteria, perhaps toward a dying friend. The very land toward which the car pointed is a land of mist, of darkness, a land of gray seas and green-black forests. A land of Chinese ghosts, Indian ghosts, and white fear. Rain covers those forests. Moss grows as carpets on the trunks of trees. Dark stone beaches are whipped by wind, by surf, by the pressing tides which lap at the land like an enormous beast—a cat perhaps—or maybe something not so agile. Something ancient, geologic, a beast blinking only once while a century passes.

Above San Francisco, here in late August, the California hills were burned brown. The coast was decorated. Enameled road signs, camper trucks, sport cars. Pretty girls wore skimpy but colorful clothing, and on the beaches they sometimes wore no clothing at all. Children were like skinny flashes of light, or like small anchors beneath balloons, or beneath bird and dragon kites pushed by the coastal breeze. They were momentarily like spirits: and there is something particularly horrible in the idea of ghosts walking at high noon and chewing hot dogs. Gulls squawked, glided, flapped, gathered popcorn, bread crusts. The coast was a spectrum of life and movement.

Beaches appear one way when you are standing on them thinking of baseball and sex and sunshine. They carry a different tone when you stand a steel deck and approach from seaward.

Just below Mendocino color began to drain from the beaches and return to the land. The coastal fog rolled across the town, across inlets and roads. It lay like a chill gray thought that comprehended the glistening hoods of cars, the tall windmills of Mendocino, then distilled as raindrops in the corners of window sills. It coated plastic menus outside restaurants, and it dimmed streetlights which were luminous disks in the late afternoon. The fog seemed a well-tailored recollection for a man on a journey toward the dead.

The Blackbird wears a watch on each wrist. One is a Mickey Mouse watch, a black mouse wearing yellow gloves, a mouse trapped in timeless semaphore as it measures seconds and days and years. On his other wrist the Blackbird wears a watch made for combat or diving. It is precise and nearly indestructible. He began wearing the watches to cover scars on his wrists where he cut them after he killed the sympathizer corporal Kim. These days the Blackbird wears the watches for other reasons.

The killing came in the wake of lunacy that happened when we were aboard ship and on station—

North and the Blackbird went ashore in the bright light of dawn. Our hare-brained executive officer had detailed them to the beach with cases of canned peaches, boxes of phosphorus grenades, three cases of ice cream mix, forty canned hams, tins of Dutch cheese, foil packets containing catsup and honey, sixteen bottles of whiskey, twenty cases of beer, boxes of laxative, fifty pounds of apples, sixteen gallons of gray enamel, four reams of U.S. Navy stationery, an enormous cooking pot, twenty pairs of arctic boots, a hand-operated adding machine, a huge world globe on an elaborately carved mahogany stand, a case of ten-gauge shotgun shells, eight dozen assorted brassieres (no one ever figured how those had ended in the supply room of a destroyer) cartons of menthol cigarettes, cases of aspirin, a bamboo birdcage, twenty gross of carpenter's pencils . . . and I do not recall the rest. The Blackbird still has the original manifest. He claims that it now hangs in a frame on his bedroom wall.

In war no one knows why anyone else does anything. The most astounding and incoherent things occur with slim reason. Maybe the exec was trying to be helpful to a brother officer in the Army. Maybe he was paying off a gambling debt. Maybe the supply officer was trying to dump inventory he did not want or could not account for. At any rate, the cargo was destined for an Army command area twenty miles into the interior.

North and the Blackbird got hold of a truck, loaded the stuff after reserving the whiskey for trading purposes, and headed inland while drinking beer. It was their first encounter with the jungle. At first they drove twenty miles an hour. The dirt tracks, which passed for a road, wound beneath dripping, sweetly-rotten smelling leaves. The sun was blocked by enormous trees. The road became more and more narrow. They suspected they had gotten the wrong directions, that they were on a road leading to nowhere. A narrow ribbon of light ran above the road. Ten miles into the interior the road began to dwindle. They feared they would no longer be able to go forward, and there was no space to turn around. They were inching forward in low gear. The Blackbird recalls that he feared he could not stand the silence or the claustrophobic grasp of the jungle.

They were captured by the U.S. Marines. The whole affair seemed a burlesque, a mouse show, a convocation orchestrated and spoken by clowns.

The marines were desperate men, but men strangely efficient and polite. They were not fools. That was proven because they were still alive. They were combat-ridden. Their faces were burned with sun. Blackened with soot. The Blackbird at first had trouble discovering which of them were white. Their faces seemed to exist only for the purpose of raising crops of hair; for all of them had beards which were chopped short by knives. Beards and mustaches existed only as circling frames for teeth. The men spoke between their teeth, or in whispers.

North remembered their seriousness and efficiency. He recalled that he had the choice of giving up the load and not dying, or giving up the load after he died. He felt vaguely violated. After all, the stolen whiskey was his by right. Now it was being taken from him.

Imagine them there: North, a Bosun Mate, the Blackbird, a Storekeeper. Two sailors accustomed to seeing death fall from the air, shells exploding on distant shores; death painting the slickness of blood across steel. Imagine them standing among crazed men in a mist-ridden jungle where death poked its snout through foliage, where blood became only a dark and soaking comment in the soil.

The marines once had been a full company. Now they amounted to a platoon, although they had native sympathizers with them. One sympathizer was little more than a boy. His nearly unpronounceable name had been distorted to Sidney, then to Sidrey. Sidrey was a tiny fellow. When he stood beside the Blackbird, even the Blackbird seemed a full-sized man.

The marines unloaded the truck. What they did not want, they stacked to one side. North figured that he and Blackbird would be left with the catsup and the gray enamel and the arctic boots. Until the last moment, neither North nor Blackbird had the least intimation that before the affair was over, they would walk three hundred miles through jungle as they carried canned peaches and the rifles of dead men.

The Blackbird vividly remembers the enemy attack. He remembers it in slow motion. He recalls watching the boy's face. Actually, he was watching Sidrey's mouth. The Blackbird was having trouble understanding the sympathizer's version of English. Blackbird watched the lips moving, listened carefully, was aware in a vague way of a growing stack of canned goods beside the skinny road.

Then the boy's face disappeared. A bullet entered the back of the skull and exploded. The Blackbird found himself carefully listening for a voice to continue from that faceless skull. He saw the inner bone of the skull. He was vaguely aware that his own face was covered with soft matter and liquid. To this day he swears that he stood there for two minutes listening for jumbled language to come pouring from the skull of a standing corpse. He did not, of course. It was a matter of a second, perhaps—no more. The sympathizer corporal Kim dived forward and knocked the Blackbird to the road. They both rolled behind a small fortress of canned peaches. Until that point the Blackbird swears he had not heard a single unusual sound. Once on the ground he heard gunfire. An enemy patrol lay in ambush.

The history of war contains thousands of futile and desperate battles fought over inconceivably stupid objectives. This battle in the jungle was as desperate as any battle ever waged, and it was between men who were mad for ham and cheese and peaches. When the firefight was over, not one carton had been hit. The Blackbird swears he was safer behind that narrow stack of canned goods than at any other time in his life.

What caused the attack? The question haunted North and Blackbird. Why would a single squad on patrol—and even owning the element of surprise—take such a desperate chance? That squad attacked a platoon of veterans in the game of killing.

The attackers were not starving. North saw whitish fat peeled away from a gut wound opened by a fragmentation grenade. The enemy belly pulsed as the man died, the belly digesting.

The marines were not starving; the enemy was not starving; and yet somehow—and North could never even speak of this— somehow the root of the battle was enormous hunger.

These marines carried no esprit de corps. Such foolishness is good enough in bars and on drill fields, not so good in a jungle. Instead they carried a rough honesty. They regarded North and the Blackbird as supercargo, as men of inexperience who would shortly die. Between the time when they would be killed and then, the two sailors could serve as carriers. The marines did not actually press the Blackbird and North into service. They simply pointed out that the truck radiator sported a bullet hole. They encouraged the Blackbird and North to discuss the matter. The two men did this as the marines buried the boy Sidrey in a shallow grave. The Bird and North could walk ten miles along a road which might sprout an enemy patrol, or they could walk with a platoon of killers while carrying goods. North recalled being furious about the choice. After all, they were supposed to be in a secured zone. They had been so certain of their safety that they left their helmets in the barge when they came ashore. They were nearly weaponless. North carried an antiquated .45 automatic.

The Blackbird, who was raised on the streets of Philadelphia, did not waste his time in anger. He foraged among the enemy dead for helmets and rifles. Then he made one of those obscure, but somehow significant, gestures for which he would become notorious. The Blackbird stood the huge globe in the middle of the road. It rested on its gorgeously carved mahogany stand. The narrow band of sunlight above the road highlighted the reliefs of the globe. Sunlight and shadow. Colored continents, green and red nations. Orange nations; blue seas.

The Blackbird put his white hat on the globe. North recalled his last sight of that road as the platoon faded into the jungle. A fresh grave lay beneath dripping branches, and above it a world globe wearing a sailor's white hat stood in silent benediction.

No one on our ship saw them for months. I was the one who found them. Then the war got in the way, and no one on the ship saw the three of us for another two months.

I can't explain the exact difference between memory and recollection. Memory is something a person consciously tries for, while recollection more or less comes unbidden. But, with recollection, it seems that you chew a little longer; maybe work harder at understanding what pushed it into your mind. It is like analyzing a dream. I thought of the problem as I drove toward Bjorn North and his demons, and as the narrow California road turned into a narrow Oregon road.

I spent the night in a gloomy beach motel on the Oregon coast. It was one of those places where the walls are in need of washing, but where blue light floods the toilet seat and gives the illusion that foul diseases are being flooded away. A narrow paper strip across the seat brags of sanitation.

Another problem with war is that men in combat assume patterns which make the civilized world ridiculous. When, for example, the main disease is bullets, no one going to a whorehouse worries about using prophylactics.

Then the men return to a sanitary world where tobacco and alcohol and drugs are supposed to be supplanted by antiseptic and good manners. One never meets good manners in battle, although one occasionally meets compassion. Men find it hard to make the switch from mortar fire to sanitary toilets.

In the jungle you are always surrounded. So is the enemy. There is no clear demarcation. It is a deadly game of hide-and-seek where the enemy will never appear before your guns. The enemy will be to one side, or at your back. Day after day, week after week, surrounded. Black men and white men develop cautious patterns of insanity. As do Orientals.

Encirclement continues when the war is over. Then the sanitary people—the ones who started the war in the first place—insist you join their illusions. "Work hard. Get ahead. Don't kill anybody. Find some way to look at children and not imagine burned flesh, empty eye sockets."

The antiseptic people insist that you be nice to the waiter who stiffs you for a dollar. They ask that you think kindly of the politicians who even now plan a war to kill your sons.

"Because," they say, "we are all in this together, my friend. Think kindly thoughts and love us."

I fight back by wielding the law. It makes a little sense to be a lawyer. Not much else does. I'm a good lawyer because I've fired rockets, because I've spent two months in the jungle.

The marines in that platoon were outlaws. In military terms

those marines were operating independently. Their commander, back at Group, could never be certain what they would do. They were roving, honed, horribly efficient. Their mission was to protect the perimeter of that large Army camp.

In practical terms they walked and killed. They were phantoms fading through the jungles, phantoms turning to the sudden heat of amazing flame when they encountered resistance. They were survivors because they killed on the basis of probability. If an old native had the bad luck to see them as they crossed a road, the old native was shot. Maybe the old person would have said nothing about their location. The marines stayed alive because they always tilted probability in their favor. They were statistical killers, more easily and intimately understandable than computers which fire rockets.

The Blackbird and North became immersed in that. If the marines regarded them as supercargo, Blackbird and North did not. They understood that if they were to survive, they would have to learn fast. The Blackbird learned almost right away.

By the time I found those marines, the Blackbird and North had seen a variety of things, done a variety of things.

It happened this way—one more part of the madness.

Our destroyer ran out of rockets. Incredible. No one had paid attention to my inventory reports. The ship mounted two banks of pom-poms that would only depress far enough to take the top off a mountain at a four-mile range. We mounted some old heat-seeking missiles, which any attack pilot old enough to shave could avoid by dropping a few flares. We had plenty of depth charges, although the enemy had no submarines. In other words, the ship was defenseless. There was lots of maple syrup in the pantry, jugs of whiskey in the captain's quarters, but, by God, there were no more rockets. The ship withdrew, hunting for a tender, a mother ship.

Before it withdrew that same idiot executive officer put me on the beach.

"You caused this," he said. "You made us run out of rockets. No rockets, no gunnery officer." He was a man with Yankee eyes, and with cheeks like marinated beef steeped in booze and tropic sun. A great leader of men. A great navigator: with slumped shoulders and a great belly and a great butt. He was the only naval officer in history who had ever crashed into a dock while pulling away from it.

"File charges," I told him.

He knew, and I knew, that if he could get me killed there would never be an inquiry. No one would ever ask why a destroyer had steamed away from an action because it was defenseless.

"Bring them sailors back," he said, "and the captain will be happy." He was pleased. "If you don't come back the exec will be happier."

I went ashore, under protest, and I was afraid.

Rumors were coming back to the ship; of two sailors who were crazier than most marines. Each of the men had shown up once at that large army base. They came in a captured truck. They drew supplies for that outlaw platoon.

The white sailor was a jolt of savage fear. He arrived unaccompanied, and he wore rotten-smelling scalp locks stitched to his shirt. He eventually went on an alcoholic binge and tore a whorehouse to pieces after bedding every woman in the place. That, of course, was not unusual. The unusual event happened before the drinking began.

The white sailor had become Asiatic, but worse than most. Usually men just mumble through convenient Oriental customs, or play at being Oriental. This sailor was sardonic. His laughter was cruel; his large teeth and flushed face were like a caricatured troll before a carnival funhouse. Before he began drinking he sat beside a Buddhist monk for three hours, sitting in what seemed complete and reverent silence. Then he stood, bowed, and shot the unsurprised and undismayed monk in the face with a .45 pistol. He left town through crowded streets and at high speed. He was indifferent to screams and thumps and rag-like, rolling bodies.

It was not, the rumors admitted, that the white sailor did unheard of things. It was simply, the rumors said, that when other men did such things they usually had some excuse, no matter how flimsy. This sailor, North, was like an animal snarling above a carcass. He seemed pressed by fear that there would be a shortage of bodies, of women, of whiskey; a shortage, in fact, of omnipotent illusions which galloped through the corridors of a mind gone wild.

But it was the black sailor who gave pause to even the most seasoned men. The black sailor arrived in the same truck, but accompanied by the sympathizer corporal Kim. The two men were efficient. They were quiet while drinking, unremarkable while bedding, and they drove carefully through crowded streets.

Where the white sailor sported scalp locks sewn to his shirt, the black sailor simply wore black feathers in his hair. The feathers were intermingled, stitched and braided, so the man's head was aruffle with black. He looked like a surprised crow.

The black sailor left live grenades with unbent pins as calling cards. The things were harmless enough, so long as no fool pulled the pin. When he left a bar, a grenade lay on the table. When he left the supply depot, a grenade lay on the supply sergeant's desk. The sailor left grenades on the beds of women. The sailor was pleasant, even courteous; and both he and the sympathizer corporal Kim seemed to think of the grenades as—not tips for service— but party favors. There was an abstract gaiety about the men that seemed to define the war as a cotillion; or a clambake. They were great friends.

I had the bad luck to find them on the day the war heated up, the day the enemy mounted a counteroffensive. An army truck dropped me, and supplies, at a rendezvous point.

There was a clash of helicopters above the jungle; a whip, whip, whip of rotors thumping like pulse. Along the roads a frightened native population streamed ahead of the enemy, while overhead the helicopters hosed the jungle with rockets and gunfire. The sounds seemed gratuitous. The flames were real. The fire sprays everywhere, along roads, or is absorbed in the dripping silence of the jungle. Occasionally a rocket hits the top of an enormous tree. When that happens a small tear appears in what seems the impenetrable umbrella of the jungle.

North saved my life, and not only once. I was green, confused, vulnerable in the shocking push and shove of forces explod-

ing around us. North was not particularly pleased to see me—
"What the hell are *you* doing here," he said—I was, after all, an
officer—but we hailed from the same ship. That called on some
loyalty that still lay curled and embryonic in North's notions of
righteousness.

There was also this: he knew that sooner or later a court-
martial was likely. It was obvious that the marines were not holding the sailors hostage. North may have protected me because I
was a lawyer. He kept me alive as council for his defense.

For the next two months North and the Blackbird were never
far from my side. We saw, and did, a number of things. "As sweet
as hell and Hallelujah," the Bird would say of those things. North
remained silent. He stopped taking scalps.

The two months were spent in retreat, circling, counter-
attack, retreat, and more circling. Somewhere, sitting in the state-
room of an aircraft carrier, a few admirals and generals may have
known the overall situation. They probably drank together, and
called each other by first names: Pete, Tom, Bob. They spoke of
strategy and women. We spoke only of tactics, and we called each
other by any vulgarity that was convenient.

Toward the end of the second month there seemed some
hope we would leave the jungle. The military situation steadied. It
much resembled what it had been when North and the Blackbird
first entered that narrow road. There were no clear lines of defense and offense. We and the enemy were once more surrounding
each other. The area was declared secure. The deadly game of
hide-and-seek continued.

At the time there seemed a second reason for hope. At the
time.

Looking back on it—as I looked back on it during the final
leg of the drive up the Washington Coast and my meeting with
North—that second hopeful reason was at the root of any horror
which dwelt in the dark forests of North's mind. It dwelt in much
of the horror that lay ancient in my own mind, a horror darker
than the wet fir forests of Washington, darker than the tumbling
black waters of the Strait of Juan de Fuca.

The second hopeful reason was this. Our ship returned to its station with a fresh bellyful of rockets. The rockets fell in the jungle and made men fearful; but mostly the rockets wrecked a little foliage, changed the smells from rotting vegetation to the sharp scent of high explosive. Once we saw them fall on a village, saw mud rising in fire, mud changed to dust, then to flame. At the time all I could really understand was that the computers still functioned.

And then—and may all Gods there are—if there are any—protect us—the rockets one day fell in a graveyard.

There were plenty of fresh graves in every graveyard of that country. The native population continued to practice its ceremonies. A part of their ritual was to erect small fences around each grave. The fences were called 'spirit fences'. Most of them were white. Most of them were made of plain wood. Some of them were ornate. The small fences kept away the hungry spirits of the dead which flew across the world in their relentless, and hopeless, and eternal quests. Or, the fences kept tormented spirits contained.

Our ship's rockets took care of the spirit fences. The spirits were released. We saw final degradation as graves were upturned, as corpses tumbled skyward in geysers of flame.

To North it was a thunderous joke. Lightning and thunder. The absurdity tickled his fancy. He laughed like a demented inquisitor. North's Protestant God was one of the Scandinavian versions, a god consorting with Valkyries. He thought it one more fine offense against one more pagan religion. He was red-faced as he laughed, although his blond eyebrows were strangely white, as white as his sun-bleached hair. Recall that North had already murdered one Buddhist monk.

To the sympathizer corporal Kim, the affair with the graveyard was another matter. All through the two-month ordeal, Kim and the Blackbird had retained their insane gaiety. They shared food. They fought well and trekked well. They worked together like fingers on the same hand. They sent the enemy to heaven or hell with impartial joy. When Kim laughed his eyes were wide and seemed almost round. He had a small mouth. When he laughed his mouth and eyes were like three flat circles of mirth across his flat face.

After the business of the graveyard Kim became morose. His eyes were heavy-lidded, and they looked toward North with an occasional flat stare. Kim no longer laughed. North laughed in defiance, but he kept his holster flap unbuckled. He was careful about which direction he pointed his back.

Why did Kim take the rockets so seriously? Was it North's laughter? At the time none of us knew. Perhaps those spirit fences had been Kim's symbolic bunker against reality. The fences might have had the same illusory protection as, say, two-inch steel plate behind which we hid on the destroyer. Neither fence nor steel plate is at all effective, if viewed sanely. The problem is that no one was sane.

Kim and the Blackbird became even closer. They often sat in silence. What Kim confided to Blackbird was unknown, because the Blackbird did not discuss it.

The final, killing act arrived on the heels of a miracle. It was a mindless miracle, true—a part of the great absurdity of battle— but a miracle which even the Old Testament Joshua would have praised.

We were caught in high grass in the middle of fields. We were crossing fields just after dawn. Our position was such that if the enemy were close he should be blinded by the rising sun.

"It's a sell out." Those were North's first words when the gunfire began, and when everyone was hitting the deck. North yelled the words before he was fully stretched on the ground with his weapon pointed. Off to the left a man screamed. An enemy voice yelled and laughed. North's face was as white as his eyebrows.

North was right. This was not an error in command. The platoon was sold. Euchred. Somebody had been consorting with the enemy. We were jammed. Pinned. Enfiladed. We were the same as dead men.

Automatic weapons opened up from under the cover of tall grass—only grass—on our left flank. Machine guns opened up from an area of jungle that curved across fields and toward the left side of our line. A narrow neck of trees jutted on our right, and from them machine guns began spouting. The gunfire was solid. It was actually mowing the grass.

Dead men. We could attempt to retreat two hundred yards across flat grassland, or we could lie pinned until the enemy brought up mortars. The machine guns searched the grass, whipped the grass. The air seemed full of flying seeds, pollen, stem heads. The weapons were working by sectors, in much the way our ship's computers worked by sectors. Our problem was that these sectors were small, and there were not many of them. North and I wiggled forward, holding grenades, trying to get in throwing distance. Stupid. Every time we moved, the grass moved. A machine gun hosed above us.

The sun lay like a carpet on the grass. I remember lying with the lip of my helmet pressed against the ground, and I was suddenly smelling soil. It was almost like I could hear movement in the soil, of insects, bacteria, growing roots.

Then the clang and bang of mortars began. Another man screamed, and for a few minutes he continued screaming. I recall thinking silly thoughts about the law. This is a divorce, I thought, a matter of community property.

And then the miracle arrived on the heavy sound of engines.

The sky was clouded with transport planes. Shadows of planes were whipping over us like shadows at a light show. It seemed that every plane owned by every air force in the world had decided to converge over those fields. There must have been enough planes that a man could step from wing to wing, walking across the sky. In less than two minutes, men—and corpses— began falling around us.

Somewhere, at an army headquarters, a general had looked at a map and seen an area of fields in a zone marked 'secured'. He ordered a low-level jump for parachute troops, a training exercise. Two thousand men dropped in about fifteen minutes; two thousand dropped into fields enfiladed by machine guns.

A corpse collapsed beside us. The morning was windless. The

chute billowed, then fell to cover the grass like a comforting thought. The dead eyes still held more excitement than surprise. There was very little left of the thing from the chest down. The aircraft engines continued pulsing, pulsing.

A living parachutist dropped on the other side of us, rolling on his back, releasing the chute and screaming. He was yelling, "Ted, Ted," and then he was yelling, "Medic, Medic." He tried to crawl over us in a desperate attempt to reach the dead man.

"Teddums is deadums," North told him, and giggled. North was hysterical with relief. Color returned to his face. The planes thumped and droned, the shadows flickered. "Load and lock, my man," North said. "Ready on the right, ready on the left, ready on the firing line . . ." North's hysteria clanged like mortars. He clung to the ground and listened to the cacophony of machine gun fire, the surprised screams, the curses. It was a shooting gallery, but the enemy could not shoot them all. It was just a matter of time. North lay flat. He began screaming vulgarities, and jokes, at the enemy. The planes droned.

"There is nothing you can do," I told the parachutist, "except to save yourself. Let the men who land behind the guns take care of it." He was a young Alaskan Indian. The physical type is easy to spot. The brown, fleshy face dropped its grief and took on fear. The boy hugged the ground. He did not even ready his weapon.

At most, it took an hour. Grenades exploded. The machine gun fire gradually dwindled. Before the last gun was silenced we heard the thumping of helicopters. They were arriving to bring men back from a successful jump. Instead they began a long and busy day carrying wounded and the dead. An incident of war. The general who ordered the action was later commended for taking out the last pockets of resistance in the area. Another incident of war.

We rose from that tall grass like resurrected men. Like men discarding the shrouds of their graves to stand confused and blinking in sunlight. Like men released to once more wander the streets of some unholy city.

Kim and the Blackbird stood. Faced each other across the

sunlit grass. Kim was calm but the Blackbird was shaking. Kim smiled, a tan face smiling without fear at a black face. Kim's smile was not apologetic. The Blackbird murmured, whispered. Kim shrugged. His weapon was resting at his side. With his free hand he pointed a finger at his chest, searching with the finger; the exact location. Nodded. The Blackbird whispered, "No." Kim smiled, insisted. The Blackbird shot Kim precisely, exactly where the finger had pointed. It was over in less than ten seconds.

We had all once more hit the deck.

"He'd ought to pay attention where he points that thing," North complained. "He could mess around and actually *kill* somebody." North's voice was whining with disbelief.

I said an incredibly stupid thing. "What are friends for," I said.

We were all shocked. Kim had asked an awful thing of the Blackbird. Yet it was easy to understand. Kim knew it was all over for him. Half of the remnants of that platoon had already figured that Kim was the betrayer. They had thought through our movements of the past few days, recognized that only a scout—Kim—could have made contact with the enemy. Kim no doubt figured it better to die quickly and with dignity, than to die in the way those marines would have killed him.

Why had Kim betrayed us? The Blackbird knew, but he was not talking. The whole affair was small and private. When the men from that platoon once more stood, viewing Kim's body lying in the grass, a few parachutists were looking our way. Then they shrugged and went about their business. One more Oriental face, one more execution; it was routine. What was not routine is that the Blackbird was passing from the insanity of battle into the permanent insanity that would hold him like a bone in a wild dog's teeth.

The Blackbird lay beside Kim all that day. Sometimes he embraced the body, but mostly he lay beside Kim as two lovers might lie beside each other in a field. It was strangely sexual, although nothing of that sort had gone on between those men. At the same time it was as wise as a living beast lying hopelessly beside a dead mate. The Blackbird held long conversations that day. He spoke to Kim, and—at least in the Blackbird's mind—Kim answered. Sometimes the two of them argued, although we only heard Blackbird's side of matters. If anyone approached them, the Blackbird raised his weapon. After the first few minutes everyone left him alone.

The Blackbird nearly died because he was left alone. As evening came on, and as the helicopters began switching on landing lights in order to find the beaten surface of the fields, it was time for us to leave. The remaining men of that platoon were being evacuated. I arranged to take my sailors back to the ship. North and I went to persuade the Blackbird. It was time to leave.

He was nearly dead when we got him. He sat astraddle Kim's body. The Blackbird had cut his wrists, and cut them with a great deal of care. The cuts were just deep enough to give a steady but not gushing flow of blood. The Blackbird was dripping the blood into the chest wound of the corpse, as though Blackbird were trying to resurrect Kim by the pouring of his own blood. He must have been at it for quite a while. The Blackbird was so weak from loss of blood that he could not struggle. He stared at us dumbly, as we stopped the blood and yelled for a medic.

Blackbird was airlifted out. He was sent to a hospital, then to a detention center while his wrists healed. He was discharged for mental disability said to exist prior to his enlistment. No pension. No disability payments. The military, which views routine destruction as a rational process, stands aghast when the subject is suicide.

For some years I received strange postcards from the Blackbird. Sometimes the only message was the drawing of a black face, a black feather, a brown face. Sometimes he drew flowers, or cactus. The postcards came from Reno, Salt Lake, Pocatello; well, the postcards came from all over the West. Once he wrote that he was teaching horses how to fight cowboys. His messages were scrawled in crayon.

And that is the history, except for a little tidying up.

I represented North at his court-martial. He received a

month's restriction to the ship, a one-half forfeiture of pay for that month. I was transferred as executive officer to a small boat basin. A reprimand went with me. My fitness reports stated that I was totally inept at logistics. The reports did admit that I knew how to fire rockets. Tidying up. In the years that followed I saw North once, on a visit he made to San Francisco. I kept in touch with the Blackbird by mail. Some vague thought of friendship, or of penance—something—kept me writing to the Blackbird.

I figured that sooner or later he would need a lawyer.

□   □   □

It was raining lightly when I passed Portland and out of Oregon, then entered the far northwest. The State of Washington seemed almost consciously intent on showing its most somber tones. Highways were beaten and slick. Dark fir forests were cut here and there with the fainter darkness of alder and madrona. The coast road ran past beaches. It took a long loop into dripping forests as it bypassed an Indian reservation.

It is a rare day, even in summer, when that coast does not get rain. Seals and sea birds appeared like spirits from the coastal mist. Huge rocks stood like ancient tombstones, water-worn testimonials to the twenty thousand years of human life and human death which have muttered through this rain. An eternity of rain existed on the roofs of cabins, and moss covered the cedar shingles of cabins like thick watchcaps. The cabins were shrouded. The land was shrouded.

In the small town the Chinese owner of a sagging and weather-worn restaurant gave me directions to North's house. The Oriental face, here, in a place wetter than the Everglades, was a small shock but not a surprise. Chinese have been on this coast for more than a century; as have Japanese and Taiwanese. The Orientals arrived as bond slaves. They were excellent workers. Enslaved Indians were not.

In late afternoon, and beneath dark and raining skies, North's house was a small beacon in the darkness of the surrounding forest. Every light in the place was glowing. The pot-holed lane to the house was overhung with branches. Water filled the ditches and in one place crossed the lane. I parked beside an old pickup that was connected to a new horse trailer. Painted on the door of the truck was a cartoon head of a surprised bird. The truck's body was a patched-together shack. It looked like a tent made of shingles; but, knowing the Blackbird, it did not leak.

I stepped from the car. There was movement at the edge of the forest.

A deep memory of movement in the jungle automatically pushed me down. I dived beside the car, onto my knees in wet soil. The pistol was packed in my luggage. Defenseless. Then, remembering where I was, and silently cursing the forest and myself, I stood back up.

There were sounds coming from the edge of the forest. A small dark figure stood beside a bulk of darkness that moved, stopped, moved. The darkness of the forest was intense, but not intense enough to cover the solid blackness of those two figures. Then a miniature spot of white, like fluorescence, darted between the two figures. It moved like a hand.

"This is no fit place," the Blackbird's voice said. "We'll be out of here in a couple of days."

He stepped from the background of the forest, leading a large black horse with white stockings. The horse was giant, but it moved light-footed and graceful. It looked stern. Wary. "Stay away from this horse," the Blackbird said conversationally, "he's a meateater."

I watched as the Blackbird loaded the horse back into the trailer, then rubbed it down. It looked likely that the horse would be more comfortable than any of us. There was enough room in that dry trailer for two horses.

The Blackbird's right hand was white, like a hand dipped in flour. He was wet. Water soaked his western hat and his jeans jacket. Water had glistened on the dark hide of the horse. In the growing darkness the only thing finally visible was that skeletal-looking hand.

"You brought a horse," I said, speaking into the darkness.

"All the way from Montana?"

"I got nothing against Montana," the Blackbird said easily. "It's just that nobody else can handle this 'un." He gestured back to the horse. "I'm saving Montana some trouble." He closed the rear of the trailer.

"I'll be along directly," he said to the horse. He turned. "You never know how much they understand," he said. "I always tell him how long it'll be."

He took off his hat. His hair was a thick braid. Feathers were interwoven in the braid; black feathers, crow, raven. The two watches looked oversize on the narrow wrists. He knocked water from the hat. The white hand was not all white. The tattooing traced along the skeletal structure. Some unknown tattoo artist was a genius. The bones seemed to lie above the surface of the hand, the flesh under the bones. The watch built for combat was a thick, low-glowing lump above the bones. His left hand was not as dark as the rest of him. Later on I would see that it was tattooed as tan as Kim's face.

"I'd rather be seeing you in San Francisco," the Blackbird said, "but since it's here I'm glad anyway." The Blackbird does not lie, and so he was glad.

"Sure," I said. "San Francisco. But since we're here..."

"C'mon to the truck. We won't be going in there for a while." He motioned toward North's house, then walked toward the truck.

It was no bad thing to sit in the cab of that truck. Smells of oil and harness and horse dung had tanned the worn seat covers. One windshield was cracked. The gearshift knob was a carved bird with a yellow cap; a yellow-headed blackbird.

"Why not," I asked, and pointed toward North's house. I looked through the rain-running windshields at the rain-covered forest. The truck cab was dry.

"The doctor figures North is going to die," Blackbird said, and he said it like a joke. "The preacher figures North is going to hell. North is sorta resisting."

"Drinking?"

"I doubt I'd want to do it sober, myself." Blackbird chuckled.

"Or maybe I would. If a man gets too crocked he'd lose all interest. You can see how that would go."

"Drinking now?"

The Blackbird laughed. "He's sitting in there with a fifth, and that blamed old .45. He's all set to shoot something. Best if it isn't us."

"Himself. Shoot himself?"

"Nope," Blackbird said. "North never did amount to much, and he sure don't amount to *that* much." The white hand rested on the gearshift. "I've heard of folks having ghosts," he said, "but I never knew a man to have a whole kyoodle of 'em."

"I told him to stay sober," I said. Then I felt like a man confessed to prudishness.

"He was sober when I got here. Minute I got here he felt real safe." The Blackbird laughed, almost giddily. "Safe," he chuckled.

"I don't know a thing about horses," I said.

"I don't know a thing about anything else," Blackbird said. "I *think* I know things. I *think* I know just *heaps*. But all I can guarantee is horses."

And then, and suddenly, we were laughing. We were hysterical with the laughter. Laughed in each other's faces. We ho-ho'ed and hee hee'd, like school girls at a slumber party. We giggled, chortled, yelped with laughter. I mentioned that there was a man in that house, a man who had saved both our lives at one time or another, a dying man. That made us laugh even harder. The Blackbird slapped his knees, slapped mine. We went yuk, yuk, and whoo, whoo. We banged with our fists on the dashboard. Tears came from the laughter. I hugged the Blackbird, as if the Bird were a solidly set post to which I could cling and not fall into a faint from the laughter.

"Maybe it's the rain," the Blackbird chuckled. "Maybe you got to either laugh or hit somebody." He wiped tears. "Fool," he said. "Our boy figures that Buddhist monk he shot is coming for him. Figures the Buddhist is bringing all his relations."

I sat giggling into the darkness and rain. Maybe death was coming to North, but not in the form of a Buddhist monk. A monk would be indifferent to all that.

"Those people have a lot of relatives," I said; and I tried to say it soberly but still had to swallow a chuckle. "North needn't worry about the Buddhist, just the next of kin."

Blackbird rolled the window. He stared toward North's house. "He'll pass out directly."

"Something that isn't funny..." I said. "This is the first time we've been together when there was no combat." It was a little surprising to think that.

The Blackbird straightened, poked a finger at the rain. "You been living too soft," he muttered, "don't let down."

North was a big man. It took a lot of whiskey to put him away. When night came on and the forest turned black, as impenetrable as slate, the Blackbird drove me, truck and horse into town. We parked between logging trucks and ate dinner in a weather worn hotel. We spoke together like brothers. People around us glanced at the Blackbird's hand and continued chewing; salmon, steak, potatoes. Loggers burped, yawned, scratched their armpits. An Indian waitress and a Chinese waiter made silent crossing patterns around the tables. Along the bar some awfully young drunks, and a few awfully old drunks, muttered to each other or gambled on punchboards. The people were indifferent to the Blackbird's hand, and to the feathers in his braided hair. I thought better of the people, if not the place. This is still the frontier—I told myself—or something very much like it.

The Blackbird had a story. He had drifted through both the Plains and Mountain West. He made his living from trading out of his truck—"I got a masterpiece inventory. I got tack and shotgun shells and gimcracks...got car parts and rope and mostly legal stuff..."—and he made his living by befriending horses no one else could handle ("I got a *way* with them.") and working an occasional rodeo ("With never no more than a busted collarbone. Not bad for a boy from Philadelphia."). He won races at county fairs, riding that giant horse. Because he won races he won bets.

"I been nosing around," the Blackbird said. "After North

commenced nursing that bottle, I exercised the horse. There's a trail back of North's house. Leads up into the jungle..." He grinned at his mistake. "Leads up into the forest."

The Blackbird chewed steak and looked like a man sitting on a thunderous joke. "The fool," he said about North. "His guilts have brought that boy back to the one place he shouldn't ever be. There's two graveyards up there. Indian and Chinese. I don't care for either one of 'em, but that Indian one is special."

The Indian graveyard was filled with elaborately carved cedar rails fashioned to imitate enormous beds. The beds surrounded the Indian graves. The dead were buried in symbolic beds.

"In pretty good shape," the Blackbird said. "Considering the rain. Looks like a sort of weird furniture store. Got slugs and moss and spiders. The beds are all decorated with them. Got these great big snails, and white worms." He chewed, slurped at coffee, and the feathers in his braided hair gleamed in the fluorescent light of the restaurant. "It all seems pretty honest when you see it that way," he said. "All them slugs and things. I got this kind of calm feeling, like death is okay. Don't like that feeling. We all know *that* ain't right."

"It might not be a bad feeling," I told him. "Sooner or later it all comes to that. Might feel all right if you could think of dying as a calm feeling."

The Blackbird looked at me in a way that said he worried about my sanity. "You been living way too easy," he said. "And you haven't seen that other graveyard." The Blackbird mopped gravy with a piece of bread. He looked round the room, looked at the Chinese waiter, then looked through the windows into the night. He checked the time on the combat watch. "Let's go see if there's anything left of our boy."

North was passed out and snoring in a chair when we entered the house. A wood fire lay dying in a fireplace. When we switched off some of the lights the fire became the focus of the room, a comment of darkened coals and ash. Outside the dripping forest was painted with darkness, a wall of darkness.

I had not seen North in a long time. Beneath the remaining

lights his face was red, his blond hair white; and breath gargled from his throat in sobbing snores. He was dressed in work clothes, booted, wearing a fisherman's coat. In his hand, which lay in his lap, the .45 automatic was dark and oiled. Except for the sleep and the stink of booze, North was a man dressed and armed for action. A man ready to rush into the night. What was he intending to do? Shoot a ghost?

Blackbird fed up the fire. "There's a couple of rooms upstairs," he said. "Take one. I'm going to sleep with the horse." He began searching the house, looking in closets. I stood watching North. The Blackbird was gone for several minutes, rummaging the kitchen and the upstairs rooms. He returned carrying an old 30-30 carbine and three kitchen knives. "I'll keep these beside me," he said. "That way if North berserks the worst he can do is smack you with a broom."

"He's that far gone?" I was ready to go back to the hotel and take a room.

Blackbird picked up the nearly empty fifth. "I figure you got time for a night's sleep," he said. "I make him to wake up come noon tomorrow." He walked to North. "Or maybe never."

The Blackbird reached toward North, took the .45 from his hand. He stood above North, a small black figure befeathered but contemplative. He seemed to be musing over the effects of history and combat and booze. Blackbird ejected the magazine from the .45, but he did not work the slide. Maybe there was a bullet in the pistol's chamber, maybe not. It all depended on how good North was at soldiering. You do not arm your weapon before you need it.

The Blackbird cocked the piece. He placed the barrel beneath North's chin, pointed at the throat. Smiled. Giggled. Laughed. Lowered the gun and turned to me.

"See this here?" He indicated North. "We came all this way to help this man."

"What are you doing," I said. "Cut the clowning."

"I'm a gambler," the Blackbird said. He watched North's flushed face, listened to the breath snorting from North's mouth. "I owe this man a debt, and he owes me. Let's leave North's ghosts to settle us up." The Blackbird stood easily, mildly humorous, re-signed to some imagined fate that I could not divine.

"It sorts out like this," the Blackbird said. "If there's a shell in this chamber, then North is gone. He's got no more problems. I'll have taken care of him and paid my debt." He looked at me. "You understand that?"

"North doesn't want to die," I said.

"Who does? He doesn't want to live in hell, either, but death or hell are all the choices this boy's got."

Flames were beginning to lick the new wood in the fireplace. The flames were tentative, searching for the easiest area of com-bustion. In my mind lay an old darkness, cut with flames. "What do you mean," I said desperately. "What do you mean, let the ghosts decide?" I was stalling for time.

The Blackbird's face gradually woke into a slow smile. Maybe a smile cannot be called historic, but this was a smile filled with memories. "I'm gonna talk here for a minute about Kim," the Blackbird said. "Kim was a man."

North snored. The new fire crackled. Night seemed pressing against the windows.

"You know why Kim contacted the enemy," Blackbird said. "You ever think about why Kim called down fire?"

"I've thought about it. They weren't good thoughts. So I stopped thinking about it."

The Blackbird gestured to the dark windows, to the black night. "That's our hearts," he said in a general way. "Our hearts were flat as those windows."

"We were little more than kids. We were in combat."

"*We* were the enemy," the Blackbird said. "We enemized everything—the dead—and the kids—and all them others." He looked down at North. "And with never a lick of respect."

The firelight was growing as fire stood brilliantly in the new logs. Shadows flickered on the wall like spirits. In my mind, deep from the darkness of my mind, figures began to walk. Then the figures began to fall, clutching guts, or grabbing at faces which were alight with flames. "Don't," I whispered. "Don't do this."—

and—I meant—don't make me recall. Just shoot North and get this over. But don't make me recall.

"We were looking at the face of something powerful," the Blackbird said, "something mighty old. We didn't even know it."

"Shoot him," I whispered. "Don't talk." I stood shocked, desperate, a willing conspirator in murder; a man betraying a friend. Echoes of rockets seemed to fill the room.

"These ghosts," the Blackbird said easily, "are hungry. They are the spirits of hunger. Kim knew. They'll never feel no peace. Ever. This here—" and he laid the pistol beside North's head— "this here is a blessing for this man. The worst it does is send him to his preacher's hell, maybe."

The words caused me to gain some self-control. After all, the Blackbird was insane. I was being persuaded by insanity. "We've already been there," I said. "Only one hell to a customer."

"Those ghosts are always lonesome. Always hungry. They are hungry for food and booze and sex. They are hungry for some kind of God somewhere. Hungry for sleep, and pretty things, and hungry for stars, and being warm." The Blackbird's voice was an incantation. "Hungry for sunlight, and kinfolk, and laughing with friends. They are starving for all those things, and blowing across the world forever, howling and hungry." He turned to me. "They scream a lot. They just wail and wail. Kim said so." He looked at North. "And they are hungry for this man. They will make him one of them, and they will still be hungry."

"Shoot," I said. The fire crackled. When rockets fall into the jungle, flame spreads. Mostly though, it goes straight up. It is a steeple of fire pointing diabolic praise at heaven. "Shoot," I whispered.

The Blackbird looked at me curiously. The black weapon glowed dull in the spectral white hand. Blackbird looked around the room, held the pistol to North's temple, paused. "It'll make a mess," he said, "and this would make a nice little house for somebody. Best if we just mess up the chair." He moved the pistol to North's chest, felt for the exact spot, and the hammer went click against an empty chamber.

The Blackbird stood looking at North. "Pretty good soldiering," he said to North, "and the ghosts have decided. They want all of you." He threw the .45 on North's lap. "I've got the magazine," he said to me. "Things'll be safe around here."

He walked to the door, turned back, looked at North. The Blackbird checked the time on one watch, then checked the time on the other. He looked more serious than he had when he pulled the trigger. "You got to understand about time," he said; and he sounded like a teacher leveling with a favorite student. "There's all the time there is, all the time."

I looked confused.

"There's the time when North is a ghost," he said, "and there's a time when he isn't. Only mystery about the whole thing was—was he actually gonna be a ghost?" The Blackbird indicated the watches. "There's the time when you weren't a lawyer and the time when you are. There's the time when you weren't born, and the time when you're dead. All them times are scampering. Right now. Like the mouse on this watch."

He opened the door, turned back, looked at North. "You shouldn't of laughed," he said to North's sleeping figure. "Everybody did bad things, but you were the man that laughed."

Blackbird stepped into the night. I crossed the room, watching through a window. In the darkness nothing could be seen but that spectral hand; and it was soon swallowed in darkness. I turned back to North, the man who still snored because he was good at soldiering. I had not expected him to be that good.

"Whatever happens," I said, "remember that the Blackbird tried to help." The thought came that sometimes it is no bad thing to be insane.

The rain stopped sometime during the night. I slept the sleep of combat; it does not allow the luxury of dreams. A part of the mind pays attention for each whisper, each footfall. I was surprised to wake refreshed, but with an accompanying depression. I had been a willing co-conspirator to murder. The murder had not happened, but that made no difference. In the gray dawn my complicity seemed a gauge of madness. I had once again discovered that when you live beside madness, you become mad.

Thick clouds blew before a freshening wind, and the forest turned from black to dark green. I made coffee, sat in the kitchen, slurped the coffee and watched through the window. North had rolled from the chair. Now he snored as he lay full length on the carpet.

No one—except Blackbird, and maybe North—could understand the gift the Blackbird had offered. In a sane world it was an insane gift. All the nicey-nice people would lift hands in horror, would cover their eyes. The sanitary people would insist that North go to a hospital, be needled and probed and sliced and oxygenated; preserved through a sort of medical embalming against whatever was killing him. The nicey people, so busy at *not* dying that they are too busy to live, would insist that North's ghosts were an aberration of psychology.

Kim knew the ghosts were real. North seemed to know it. That was enough to justify, and give praise to, the Blackbird's action. Because insanity causes its own reality. If the ghosts were real to North—and they were clearly more real than most people's sense of their Gods—then the ghosts were real.

The Blackbird appeared on horseback. The figures emerged in the lane. They were figures of black on black. It was hard to understand how a man from the slums of Philadelphia could gain complete wisdom of horses. Yet Blackbird looked knitted, not sculptured; and he was of a single piece with that horse—a painting—art—or this: he looked somehow like the dreams of men. The primitive energy, and the unconscious power of that man on that horse made him look the way all of us have *wished* we could when we were young.

When he broke into a brief run, the horse stretched like a wave. It was agile and godlike. I wondered how the Blackbird could even get someone to bet against him when he raced such a horse. He rode to the house. He tied the horse to a post which held up a sagging porch roof. I expected him to enter the house. Instead, he leaned against the post and spoke to the horse. He seemed to be having a conversation. A flicker of memory spread painful fingers in my mind, a memory of the Blackbird lying beside Kim's corpse, conversing.

After an hour, several things happened at once. I called my office. A strange voice answered. Miss Molly was not at work, the voice said. The voice claimed it belonged to some temporary helper service. I felt slight indignation.

Miss Molly, the voice said, was tending her father who was ill.

"Are you a person," I asked. "I'm not talking to a computer?"

The voice gave a name. Cynthia Seymour or Lydia Claymore. Something. Then, in sanitary tones, the voice said *Mrs.* Claymore or Seymour.

"Not *Mrs.* Computer?" It was not a sarcastic question.

The voice sniffed.

"This is the boss," I recall muttering. "Take messages until Molly returns. Do nothing else. Don't even open mail."

The voice advised me that temporary helper people were skillfully trained.

As this was going on, North began to thrash around. Then he began to moan. The Blackbird finished speaking to the horse. He drifted into the kitchen and headed for the coffeepot.

"Open mail if you must," I told the voice. "Flush the toilet when necessary. But don't *do* anything. Make no decisions." I hung up with an uneasy feeling. Reality and unreality kept shifting in my mind.

North handled his hangover with a good deal of skill. He bumbled into the kitchen, poured coffee and orange juice and water and beer. He sipped the coffee, gulped from the glasses, and his pale Scandinavian face was a portrait that would frighten a coroner. The face seemed washed by rain. Death was painted in the eyes. The cheeks sagged with death, and death smoothed his already smooth forehead. His hands trembled. The coffee cup clicked against his teeth. When he smiled—and, incredibly, he did smile—the smile was like a flicker of vanishing life swallowed in the death mask of that face.

"Couple more beers," he said, "and this mess will get

121

straight." He looked at me like a man judging a car he might buy, like a man about to kick tires; a man thinking of a deal. "Thanks for making the trip." His voice was half-humorous, deprecating, and hung over. "You drove right into hell's half-acre."

"You're gonna throw up," the Blackbird said. "Can't mix that much juice with that much beer."

"That's why I'm doing it. Cleans the system." North seemed trying to ignore the Blackbird. He seemed nearly apologetic.

"It's your throw up," the Blackbird said. "Just point it where it don't get controversial."

The Blackbird reached in his shirt pocket. He threw the loaded .45 magazine on the table. "Next time mind your manners," he said.

"It got that bad?" North slugged juice, slugged beer.

We three ex-warriors sat around a kitchen table that was covered with green oilcloth. The .45 magazine lay on the table. The Blackbird flicked it hard with an index finger. The magazine spun, pointed toward North. "Spin the bottle," the Blackbird said. "You're one down." Blackbird spun the magazine again. "You're one down," he told me. He looked at North.

"We can't be having any lies around here," he said. "I tried to shoot you last night." The Blackbird's face is proportioned to the rest of him, which means it is small. The forehead bulges slightly, but the lips are thin. The voice coming from those lips was conversational.

North looked at me, then at Blackbird. His water-smooth face was dull and unsurprised. Gray light from the kitchen window glowed softly on the copper bullet that pressed against the top lip of the magazine.

"You must not of tried very hard," North said. "Not sure what I think about you fouling up." He placed pale hands on the table, pushed himself into standing position. "Juice is doing its good work. I'll be right back." He headed for the bathroom.

North was never a stupid man. Although cunning, he had no great reputation for lying. He was dying. His face was a shroud behind which countless and awful emotions must have already fought. It seemed to me that he was handling matters pretty well.

Outside the horse stomped, seemed sighing to itself.

"They know," the Blackbird said about the horse. "That one has wanted no part of this since we got here."

The room actually became darker when North returned. Clouds blew in layers. Up there in a gusty firmament, clouds were painting the forest with darkness.

"It'll breeze like this. Come mid-afternoon it will commence to blow. Then we'll get a couple days of broken clouds." North took his seat at the table. Sipped beer. "The Blackbird hates this place," he said to me, and he spoke as if Blackbird was not sitting beside him. "It's home," he said. "I fished these waters since I was a kid. A man ought to be allowed to die at home."

The horse made snuffling noises. Then it gave a low whinny. Blackbird stood. "You'd be better off doing it in St. Louis," he said. He walked to the door. "His dander is up," he said about the horse. "I've got to level that poor fella out, or he'll drag the house down." He stepped outside.

"What is the problem," I asked North. "You said over the phone that you needed a safe place to die."

"Spirit fences," North said. "It's a long story."

It was not a particularly long story. In the last century Chinese moved in and caused a graveyard. They did not mean to do it, but they had no idea that they were enlisted as bond slaves to work at processing lime. In those days the work was cruel. Their death rate was appalling. They were buried in that graveyard, and with little hope that their bones would ever be returned to China.

"Folks around here," North said, "never paid it any mind. That graveyard sat there for seventy years. The fences would decay, and somebody would fix them. Folks here pretty much mind their own business. The Chinese stay to themselves and do Chinese things. Blackbird says I shouldn't of come home, but Chinese never had any power around here before."

Outside in the narrow clearing, the Blackbird was exercising the horse. Blackbird had the horse on a long tether. The horse was galloping or trotting—or whatever horses do—in a wide circle. The black animal seemed to blend in, then flash from, the black spaces of the forest. The white stockings moved brilliantly, as accurate as the Blackbird's hands.

North still looked pale. But now he was no longer in resigned control. His hands were shaking again. "I never did anything to those people," he said. "I never tore up those graves."

Two decades before, at a time when North and Blackbird and I were in the jungle, satanic cults in San Francisco began paying a hundred dollars apiece for human skulls.

"Nobody around here did it," North said. "Maybe some people from Oregon. Maybe some San Francisco people."

"So the fences are down again." Feelings of fire, of rocketry, lay in my mind. Beyond the windows the black horse trotted like a circus horse. Insanity seemed the only normal way of looking at things. I envied the Blackbird.

"It isn't just the fences," North said. "The grave robbers didn't even backfill. Bones exposed. It's all covered with fir needles now, but the graves are holes. Water standing in some." North looked absolutely indignant. "I had nothing to do with it. I wasn't even *around* here at the time."

He looked at me, and then there was supplication in the look. There was also cunning. "I killed a monk," he said. "That guy is coming for me. I hear them up there whispering and squalling. They wail. They do it around the house at night." North was trying to speak matter-of-fact, but his voice trembled and so did his hands.

"That monk did not have to die," I said. "He was proving a point. You saw monks over there. Sometimes they sat in the paths of tanks. You saw the tanks move into a higher gear. That monk was protesting."

Beyond the windows the black horse circled, circled, as though it were the second hand on an enormous watch.

"I was the guy that let him do it." North popped open another can of beer, looked at the beer can. "You don't get the D.T.s until you *stop* drinking," he explained. "It ain't D.T.s. It's real voices, or at least I think so. And that's why I asked you guys here," he said. "The Blackbird is insane. You are sane. I need some other ways of seeing this, because my judgment is gone."

The man looked pitiful. He was for every intent and purpose dead. The dark skies beyond the window were a frame for a face that was already ghostly. I wished I could get him so drunk the alcohol would kill him. The thought came and left.

"The spirits start wailing at sunset," North said. "At least *I* can hear them. If you, and if Blackbird, *both* hear them, then God help me." He tried to shrug, then drank instead. "My only other chance is to take my boat into deep water and drown." He tapped a pale finger on the green oilcloth. "Be a shame," he said. "There's a couple of young fellows around here could use that boat." The look of cunning did not leave his face. North made me feel that he was running a confidence game, but I could not tell what the game was.

"Don't be so sure that I am sane." It was the only honest reply I could think of. "I was all right before I got here." Then I thought of something. "Why didn't the grave robbers tear up the Indian graveyard? Blackbird told me."

"When you see it you'll *feel* why," North said.

The Indian graveyard explained itself better than North, or even Blackbird, could explain. We passed it as we ascended to the Chinese graveyard. But that happened later on, toward sunset.

North drank beer, forced down some food, and slept. Blackbird did minor work on his truck. When he opened the door of the shack-like truck body, the first thing visible was a row of rifles. "Make a lot of money swapping guns and stuff," Blackbird said.

When I approached the horse, it struck forward with a front hoof. The strike was sharp, deft; and the hoof smacked the ground like a hammer.

"He won't make friends," the Blackbird told me. "Don't get stupid and walk behind him."

I had never looked *carefully* at a horse before. This animal showed me nothing about horses, only something about itself. It was as precise as a hawk. It carried the energy and power that can focus so quickly in huge animals. I imagined this horse fighting a grizzly, and could see no end to such a fight; at least no ending which would not leave both beasts dead. On some animal level, this horse was as frightening as elemental force—strong winds, or storms, gale force, volcanic.

"He don't much get along with other horses, either." The Blackbird was cleaning spark plugs. Grease from the engine stained his hands. The white hand floated above the engine, deft in the shadowed compartment. "He's not even much of a ladies' man."

Then movement began in the forest. At least it seemed that movement was going on in there. I no longer trusted my sanity, or, insanity.

"I expect it's Indian ghost stuff," the Blackbird said. "Goes on all the time in Montana. Don't give it a nevermind." Blackbird worked with his back to the forest. He was actually humming as he tightened spark plugs.

Movement in the jungle is almost always felt, not seen. When you watch for it, you may be sure you will not see it. Movement in the jungle is picked up sometimes at the edge of vision. More often it is picked up by a feeling in the belly, or a chill that starts in the spine. Twice during the afternoon I nearly hit the deck, expecting the rake of gunfire.

The Blackbird finished with the spark plugs. He crawled beneath the truck. "I told you not to let down," he said, "but man, you are starting to fly. Don't get too high." His voice echoed, and the wind that North had predicted was beginning as a light breeze. "It pays to pay attention, but not to that forest," Blackbird said.

Memories and compulsions were congregating. For years I had discarded thoughts, reasoned out my position on bad memories. Now I pulled my pistol from the luggage. A little peashooter .38 of the kind favored by judges and attorneys. There are a lot of these snub-noses all through the law business. We pretend they don't exist. But then, we try divorces and assaults and sanity hearings; and we pretend that human emotions are objective—that for the purpose of law, emotions do not exist. We thus own .38s.

A part of my mind knew it was gripped by old madness, but the madness had its own genius. It kept picking up movement in the forest.

"If it *is* Chinese," the Blackbird said, "I doubt they're after you. If you get too wired, you'll get all wore out." His voice echoed from beneath the truck. He was talking to himself. "Ought to get another ten thousand miles from this clutch . . . old truck . . . don't owe me nothing."

In mid-afternoon the wind picked up and blew steadily. The forest came alive. Fir tops and cedar tops moved a hundred feet above our heads. Spatters of rain colored them. The Blackbird finished fooling with the truck. North stepped from his house. He was booted, dressed in work clothes, and wore an old down jacket.

"This is August," the Blackbird said. "Don't it ever, *ever* get warm around here?"

"Happens sometimes," North said. "But not so often you come to expect it." He looked at me, at the way I was dressed. "Pretty dandy outfit," he said. "There's old coats and stuff hanging in the pantry." North looked at the forest. The treetops still moved. Lower, in the darkness, the movement now seemed random; like nearly invisible targets popping up and down at a shooting gallery. "Go away," he said to the forest. His voice was trembling. "You see that," he said to the Blackbird. "Tell me you don't see that."

Blackbird leaned against his truck. On the door of the truck, the picture of the surprised bird seemed suddenly amusing. I could imagine a time when Blackbird had painted the picture, could imagine him chuckling as he laughed at himself.

"I'm with a bunch of crazies," Blackbird said. "You guys are spooked. The horse is spooked. You crazies have gone and gotten the forest spooked. Of course I see it. Why not?"

"I won't swear that I see it," I told North, "but if I *do* see it, then it's been going on for quite a while."

"How can a man be dying when he don't even feel hurt," North said. "I walk as good as ever. Got no pain in the gut." He seemed trying to convince himself that the whole business was a charade. He pulled the .45 from a jacket pocket and worked the slide. He placed the pistol to his face and looked down the barrel. "Hello, old friend," he said to the pistol, "you want to take another ride?"

"Hard to shoot yourself in the nose with a .45," the Blackbird said conversationally. "You about have to tape down that rear safety."

"I got flexible hands," North said. North spun, crouched and let off a shot into the forest. The boom of the heavy pistol engulfed the clearing, was swallowed in the forest. North let off another shot. The forest stood dark, unmoved, but containing movement.

The horse stomped. Whinnied. It tugged hard at reins tied to the porch. The porch roof shook.

"You do that again," the Blackbird said, "and you don't need to worry about no Chinese." He moved across the clearing, birdlike, a flicker of dark light. He stood by the horse's head, talking to the horse.

"You might be better off drowning," I said to North. "All three of us have lost our senses."

North looked at the forest. "It will be sunset in an hour. Might as well get it over with." He shucked the magazine, then shucked the shell in the chamber. He reloaded the shell to the magazine. He was stalling, intentionally wasting time. I clucked and cautioned, while Blackbird complained. North went to the house, insisted that we eat. He protested that we must hurry, and then held back.

When we finally entered the forest, North led. I followed. The Blackbird walked at the rear. He led the horse.

North complained bitterly about the horse. The Blackbird told him that the horse was spooked, that it was North's fault; and if North could not handle it, the Blackbird would fix matters so that North *could* handle it. We carried waterproof flashlights, and the Blackbird carried a small duffle. The horse carried a pack. By the time we returned, the forest would be wrapped in night.

The gradually rising trail was wide. With care, two men might walk it side by side. "It narrows after the Indian graveyard,"

North said.

No description could really prepare me for that graveyard. It was scattered across the face of the hill. Trees were thinned. Large, grandfather trees rose into the wind and blowing mist. The color was red, russet from cedar which towered into the decaying daylight. Red, like the fur of a wet fox, or the soft auburn of decaying maple leaves.

The graveyard was a grove in which tangles of salal and vine maple crisscrossed in flowing patterns. Wind moved through the leaves, although this deep in the forest the wind was shattered and inconstant. High in the tops of trees the wind was steady, and it was blowing a gale.

Headstones leaned, or had fallen flat. The bed-like structures—and some of them ornate—glistened with the rusty color of red cedar. It was not like a furniture store at all. The enormous beds were at many angles and distances. They were not in rows, although where families were buried some were in clusters. Cedar and fir boughs lay as fresh decorations on the ground, or across the enormous beds. It seemed that the storm was ornamenting the graveyard as it tugged branches from trees and dropped them into the forest.

"You feel it?" the Blackbird was talking to me, or to the horse.

"A dead man could feel it," I whispered.

Power lay calmly across the graveyard. The power was so evident, so serene, that even if my mind were not in a frenzy I would still feel the power. In fact, as the power became omnipotent my frenzy faded. Tranquility. Calm. Peace. Nothing foul could enter here.

North was becoming nervous. I could not understand why.

"It's a trick," he said, and seemed to be speaking to the forest. "A man dies here and you send ravens, don't you? Don't you?" He stopped, looked back at me and Blackbird.

"Don't be fooled," he said. "I know Indians, know their ways. They control ravens and crows, and they get fancy on revenge." His face was pale in the gathering dark, a white moon of a face rising against the red background of the graveyard. "You feel it waiting there? Feel it waiting? They control owls and rats and anything that bites."

"What did you ever do to Indians?" The Blackbird was actually grinning. The white hand rested on the horse's neck as we stopped. The white hand gestured, seemed floating toward the graveyard. "Indians don't care about you. Listen to how quiet it is. Just *hear* how much they don't care about you."

"People experimented," North said. "Back in the old days. These Indians have got cousins laid out here and up above. There's Chinese Indians, but no Indian Chinese, because"—and he breathed in sobbing snorts, fear ridden, and finally yelling—"because there wasn't no Chinese *women*." To North the matter was fantastically important. It was easy to see just how far his fear and his fantasies had carried him.

"I know lots about Indians." The Blackbird tried to answer seriously, tried not to giggle. "These people are tending their own fences. You're just one more crazy white man. Don't mean nothin' to them." Blackbird dropped his hand, urged the horse forward. "Get along," he said to me and North, "or I'll let go of these reins."

The graveyard was a quiet presence at our backs as we climbed. I followed North, knowing now that he was insane with his fear; a gulf of fear, a chasm. I followed him and waited for him to stumble, to fall, to plead to some Scandinavian god—to pray for storms or the sanctuary of crosses, of angel's wings—a prayer in stained glass, a prayer for burial inside a church.

The trail narrowed. Low-sweeping fir and maple branches brushed the horse's flanks. The strip of sky above the trail was red and distant, a narrow band above a land of wind and growing darkness. North stumbled forward. Movement began in the forest.

I paused, looked back down the trail. The Indian graveyard was swallowed by trees and encroaching darkness.

"You see that," North whispered. "You see it."

"I see it," I said, and I was whispering as well. The movement was as deft as the flicker of bat wings, but it was a movement of pale shadows. It appeared and disappeared right on the edge of vision. If the Blackbird's white hand were magic; if it could suddenly appear and disappear in all of the places where eyes were not looking, then that would describe the shadows.

"Whoa up," Blackbird said.

The horse was not shying, but the horse was focused. It looked the way a horse must look just before a race. The animal was huge. A great dark bulk filling the narrow trail. Its breath was heavy, the sound like a promise of power layering the darkness and the red gloom of the trail. If the horse decided to break, the Blackbird would be flung like a wadded piece of carbon paper. North and I could probably not dive from the trail quickly enough. We would be trampled.

"No talk," the Blackbird said. "I have to get this poor fellow to that clearing. The trail has got him clastrophobied. Quick and quiet. You people know what to do. You been in the jungle."

The word 'jungle' hung like a sudden fury in my mind. Jungle. My pattern of movement changed. Which is to say, I accepted the sanity of an old madness. In combat there is no sanity, only useful ways of being insane. Insanity is the only way to survive, and insanity forces its own patterns of movement.

We went rapidly up that trail and my feet were silent. My feet knew where to place themselves. My feet did not kick branches; pebbles. They did not skid on wet soil. Jungle. Combat.

We entered the Chinese graveyard more silently than whispers. Light drained from the forest, like a riptide between rocks. The sun must already be on the horizon. I memorized the terrain, because my mind was framed for combat.

There was no peace here. Only violation. In this graveyard there was a state of war.

Pale remnants of spirit fences rose crazily on broken angles above the forest debris. Graves stood nearly erect on the steep hillside, as if the dead had been buried on deliberately uncomfortable angles. The excavated graves were like empty faces, stripped bones. The hill was so steep one imagined that dead men had stood in congregations. It was a big graveyard, a lot larger than the

Indian graveyard. The Chinese had been in these parts for a hundred years, more or less; and the Indians for twenty thousand—and yet this was a graveyard which seemed as large as the antiquity of all suffering.

"That's why the skulls survived, why they were worth digging," I murmured. "The hillside graves drain. That's a mostly dry hillside in the middle of a rain forest." My insanity was doing its combat-figuring, estimating situations, figuring escape routes.

Some of the more-favored graves were situated along breaks in the hill. When they were interred, the corpses had been laid flat. Now stagnant water stood in those torn graves. In the decay—of light and the decaying putridity of stagnant water and debris—total darkness would seem a blessing.

"No matter your fear," I whispered to North, "nothing makes it right for you to have brought us here. Man, of all places on earth, this is the place where you should *not* be."

Spirit fences are not huge. Many are no taller than the ornamental fences gardeners place around their flowers. The power of the fence is the power of symbol; and here, the symbols were a rampage of killed voices. The symbols denoted the death of delicacy, of faith, of love, trust, respect, honor, memory. Some of the fences were intricately carved. I directed my flashlight here, there. A fragment lay almost at my feet (was I standing on a grave?) and the fragment—four or five inches of paint-flaked and faded scrap wood—carried such finite and patient carving that it represented years of skill and hours of work.

The flashlight was not yet fully effective. Enough natural light remained that the flashlight beam was diffused. I clung to the light. In this place it was more precious than fire, weapons, food. In this place it meant survival. A way to get out.

"Pretty quick now," North whispered. His voice trembled. "I pray to God that I hear those voices just because of the D.T.s, or just from being crazy. Maybe you guys won't hear them." His voice sounded as if he tried to be sincere, but was making a bad job of it.

Blackbird stood silent. He was memorizing the terrain.

There were no trees in the graveyard, except for a few old snags. The wind blew over the lip of the surrounding forest. It scoured at the violated graves.

The chaos of a battlefield comes not from corpses, but from disarray. Trees are broken—bodies are broken as well—but it is the shattered vegetation and the shattered works of men that make the chaos. I once saw explosions in a train carrying passengers and produce. I saw broken leaves of vegetables, the red pulp of tomatoes washing ruptured steel, and newspapers rising from a club car carried like spirits on the wind. The papers rose and circled and circled in a flume of fire.

"Folks say I'm crazy," the Blackbird murmured to the horse. The horse stood silent, nearly calm after the ascent. I had the sudden belief that the horse was listening to Blackbird's explanation, and that the horse understood. "Maybe I am," the Blackbird said, "but I ain't crazy now. We get to a place like this and the Bird knows the territory."

North's hand caressed the useless .45. "It's starting."

Only a memory of light remained. The forest was black as the Blackbird's skin, and, like the Blackbird, the forest was alive. The wind was a voice, and it pressed high above our heads as if it swept all light toward caverns at the end of the world.

The movement was no longer on the edge of vision. It was no longer entirely in the forest. We watched the movement become a fragmented wave reaching almost timidly across the graveyard, a wave of white exhausting itself like surf. The whiteness was not exactly like flickers of light. It seemed, almost, like the absence of darkness. At the same time, it became illumination when it touched the broken point of a spirit fence, or when it flashed as pale phosphorescence in the hollow face of a grave. In my imagination—in the acceptance of a mind that was now in combat—it seemed that there was movement among the graves.

The darkness was complete. North stood beside me, and all that could be seen of him was a smudge of paleness—white face, blond hair. The Blackbird stood ten paces away. All I could see was his white hand raised and resting on the neck of the now-invisible horse. I heard breathing—my own, the horse, the Blackbird—and the panting breath of North.

When the voices began they were not so alarming as the wind. It was impossible to say when they began. They were faint. The mind accepted that they had been there all along, or that they approached from great distance. The voices were like the babel of a public market, or like the disjointed buzz and bustle of a crowded street. As they increased only slightly, the imagination placed a face behind each voice, and the imagination was quelled. So many faces would fill the forest, obscure even the wind, obscure the sky. Faces. Oriental.

"Aw Kim," the Blackbird said, "no man. Aw no."

The Blackbird's voice trembled, but not with fear. No man in the world was in better control than the Blackbird, and now his voice was alive with grief.

"Aw my God," he said, "they are blind. On top of everything else."

His voice sounded as if he were screaming inside, although when he spoke to North it was in a low mutter. "I should kill you and let them have you," he said to North. "There's things a man ought not to know. You just made me know one of those things."

The voices grew louder.

"I can't stand to hear it," the Blackbird said, and he was talking to Kim. "Man, don't do this."

"I reckon he can't help it," North said. There was something peculiar, something cruel in North's voice. It was a voice of fear—but more—it was the voice of combat. The babel changed. At first it was impossible to say how the voices were modulating. It was only possible to recoil from the sounds of awful sorrow. The voices were intertwined, yet individually as distinct as each thread of a spiderweb. The voices wailed, were like a tapestry of sound; and each thread was dyed in the colors of sorrow. Sound was white, thin red, like watered blood. The cries knit in the shroud of darkness.

How can an insane man go crazy, I thought—and the voices began to wail. The wails spoke of every hunger that has ever tormented the human heart.

Hunger for food and booze and sex. Hunger for some kind of God somewhere. Hunger for sleep, and pretty things, and hunger for stars and being warm. Hunger for sunlight, and kinfolk, and laughing with friends. . . .

"If you're talking to Kim," North said to the Blackbird, "then tell him I want to make a deal."

"It isn't Kim," the Blackbird said in a low voice that carried all the horror of a scream. "It's what Kim *was* when he was killing. All the rest of him's been *eaten . . .*" Then the Blackbird choked off his words. The white hand disappeared into darkness. Sounds of the zipper on his duffle bag, the muffled sounds of steel bumping steel; these said that the Blackbird was armed.

"Lawyer man," Blackbird said, "you better find yourself a ditch somewhere."

I paused. Beside me North hesitated, then moved. He grabbed at my arm, just as I moved in the opposite direction. I pulled away, hit the deck, and rolled.

The pitch of the wailing rose and blanketed the night. Flashes of luminescence were rushing from the interior of the forest. The graveyard was filled with dancing and erratic points of light. It was like being stunned, the brain crashing about in darts and lasers of light. I rolled downhill. There was no cover. A small mound of earth stopped my movement. A grave, perhaps. Most likely it was a rain-beaten pile of soil, a mound between graves. It had been piled by the grave robbers.

"Try it out, baby," the Blackbird said to North. "Let's see how good you are." The Blackbird chuckled. "You conniving fool. Thought to trick the Bird. Up here in the dark with that swatty old .45. How'd you come to such a mess?"

Blackbird's voice seemed here, there, moving in the darkness. The horse was also moving, but only its breath was audible. It moved silent-footed, the way war horses had been trained back in the nineteenth century. When the Blackbird stopped speaking I had the feeling that he was himself a spirit. He could be standing three feet from me, and I would not know.

"Turn on your light," North said. "I can't figure what you're talking about." His voice was full of his lie. I searched for him in the darkness. Was it illusion? I could see the points of light, but they did not illuminate. North and the Blackbird were invisible.

"You turn on *your* light." The Blackbird chuckled. He was very close. Within eight or ten paces. There was a slight rustle as he moved away.

"Try not to get dead, lawyer man." The Blackbird's voice diminished as he moved away. "You die around this here mess and you get stripped. What will be left is what's holding that pistol."

The .38 was in my hand. The old patterns were automatic. I had armed myself even while rolling for cover.

"Ought we take him now," the Blackbird asked, "or ought we sweat him that least little bit?" Blackbird was not speaking to me, but to the horse.

"You got this wrong." North's voice came from a different position. He was now uphill and to the left.

I was not confused about where to point my weapon, only confused about why it pointed at North. Then realization came among the scattering points of light.

Gods of Thunder. Valkyries. Cathedrals. Burial in the church. The sacrificial lamb. *Sacrifice.*

"Brought us up here to kill us," Blackbird said to the horse. "Thought he could trade two for one, maybe. Trade off his friends." The Blackbird's voice became cruel. "Kim," he said, "shut down your light show. Let it be blacker than black, and tell your boys to wash up for supper."

The whiteness faded. The wails faded. Only the voice of the wind sang high above the totality of darkness.

"Using my left hand to toss this," the Blackbird said, and he was either talking to the horse or to Kim. "Using the brown hand, the Asiatic hand to fling this here."

His voice was covered by the huge thump of an explosion in the forest. Heat from the grenade flew red into the wet fir needles. The thump vibrated across the graveyard, and the explosion was red as a furnace. In the brief light of the explosion fir needles were seared. Branches were torn and thrown. The smell of the explosive shoved across the graveyard like a tide.

"A bag of grenades is a nice thing," the Blackbird said. "Have a lot of fun with a bag of grenades."

"Put the gun down," I said to North, and was moving even while I spoke. "If it's a mistake, then put the gun down." I rolled sideways, then inched downhill toward the forest.

Another grenade exploded. Blackbird was not throwing them into the graveyard. The explosion thumped in the forest. "I got a little H.E. here," the Blackbird said. "Wanna try some plastic?"

It was a waiting game. The night was like the depths of a cave. High overhead the wind seemed to be moving mountains of darkness toward the graveyard. Deep. Impenetrable. The wind was an enormous carrion crow, a raven; spreading wings of darkness.

When the plastic flashed it was sharp, white, brilliant. Blackbird had attached the plastic to the trunk of a large fir. The graveyard appeared as in a flash photograph, lighted to show North crouched a hundred feet up the hill and among the graves— Blackbird invisible—the horse invisible—somewhere in the forest.

I chanced a shot with that pathetic little .38. North wheeled and emptied the magazine in my direction. We were both stunned by the light, our ears cracking with the slap of the explosion. Before North's last round crashed beside me, shattering an already broken spirit fence, the rush of the blasted fir was like an exclamation. The tree thumped, bounced, thumped again.

North had lost none of his ability with that pistol. A .45 in the hands of most men is not particularly dangerous, not at a hundred feet—like throwing huge stones—but North was good with it. His fire was not erratic. It was called 'searching fire', and it was statistical. He carefully placed the rounds to cover the area where he last saw me. There was the unmistakable sound of the pistol's slide. North had loaded another magazine.

"Best to quit playin' around," Blackbird drawled to the horse. "That lawyer's gonna get his fool-self killed."

I rolled further. Backed up. Edged toward the forest.

"Keep it shut," the Blackbird whispered to me. He was within a few feet, and astride the horse. His whisper was covered by the wind. "Let one off in two minutes. Wait two minutes. Do it again." He passed me two grenades. "Got to keep him outta the forest," he whispered.

If North got into the forest he need only wait for our flashlights as we tried to leave the graveyard, or wait for daylight to ambush us.

"Got a little timer down there," the Blackbird said. "It all comes together in six minutes." He disappeared into the darkness. The silent horse was moving awfully fast among the graves. Even that silent-moving horse could not avoid some sound on that steep slope.

A cruel and wonderful joy accompanied those grenades. They nestled in my hands like children. They were more beloved than any woman. The beautiful weight of the things; heavy as sexual urgency, promissory as good books, good whiskey—My God, I thought, *this* is what I am—*This.* No madness was so great that it could obscure the beauty of *this*—these sane and perfectly sculptured grenades.

I loved the Blackbird. I loved him like I have never loved a woman. He was my comrade, my friend. He trusted me. Our lives were in each other's hands.

I arched the first grenade back into the forest. It bounced from a tree, exploded in a small gully, a culvert, a stagnant pool, a hidden grave; something. Water and steam rose into the trees like a puff from the breath of hell. North's pistol exploded. One round. The muzzle flash was above me, and now to the right. North was firing across the hill, at some sound of the climbing horse.

The bullet clacked as it hit the saddle or stirrup or pack. The horse screamed, and the scream rose in the wind like the voice of a frightened child. The horse sobbed. Quieted. It was breathing in huge, sucking breaths.

"Aw man," the Blackbird said, "now I'm gonna have to kill you twice." He was moving fast, and away from the horse. "You better shoot," he said to North, "because the Bird is gonna hurt you."

The Blackbird was intentionally drawing fire. It made no sense, unless the Bird was trying to keep North on the hill. Maybe he was trying to draw North's fire away from the horse. North emptied the magazine into the darkness, toward the Blackbird's voice.

I fired once, just above and behind the pistol flash.

"Dead," the Blackbird said. "North is deadums."

There was the sound of North loading another magazine. I could not believe that I had missed him. My combat sense said that I had *not* missed. I waited for the heavy breathing of a wounded man. I waited for his desperate fire.

Maybe he was only nicked, was moving quickly for the forest. I searched, found a clod of wet soil and threw it to the right. Silence. Darkness. Wind. When I threw the second grenade it flashed among shrubbery to the right and at the edge of the forest.

North fired two rounds of random fire. In throwing to the left, then to the right, I had allowed him to bracket me. North was good—nobody could deny that he was good—and he was apparently unwounded. He was as highwired on combat as any of us. His fire was random, but his instincts were tuned. The bullets slapped within two or three feet of my position. He was using a lot of ammunition. He must have come prepared to fight a war.

The second grenade was expended. Two minutes remained.

Silence. Darkness. Wind. The wails of the spirits were abated, hushed; yet the presence—or maybe the awful memory of Kim with a bloody chest—the awful memory of the Blackbird dripping his own blood into the wound—hovered above the graveyard; and the silence was momentous with subdued sighs, sobs, weeping.

Oh, he was crazy. Oh that Blackbird was *crazy.* I truly loved how truly crazy he was, because when the timer went off the darkness became a shattered parenthesis for light.

No sane man would be carrying grenades and fireworks.

Grenades, maybe. Fireworks, no. Blackbird, both.

I hit the deck as strings of firecrackers began to rattle like small arms fire. The wind dipped around them. The stink of black powder spread before the twinkling explosions. The wind layered it across the graves. The explosions looked like blasts from a congregation of rifles. There was a long, rapid running fuse burning down there. It was a hot glow running a thin line of red—strangely buglike—a ladybug—through the darkness. Firecrackers popped around a nearly intact spirit fence which stood like skeletal legs. On the ornately carved pickets of the fence two pinwheels began twirling like a cartoon automobile hell bent for nowhere. The pinwheels threw gay little twinkles of red; a comedy, a mouse show. Mickey.

The fuse ran. A skyrocket rose, arced, pointed into the graveyard.

"Hit him," the Blackbird yelled. "Hit him, hit him, hit him."

I twisted toward North. The rocket splatted, threw fire in sprays, threw red sparkles. North was moving from a crouch. I snapped off a shot as he hit and rolled.

"No," I muttered, "not that. Not even you..." and I was screaming at North... "you are better off in hell than doing what you've done."

North had taken cover in an excavated grave. A macabre foxhole.

Behind me the rattle died away, and the colors fell as the pinwheels sputtered and died. I took careful aim at the nearly hidden figure of North. Fired. Two shots remained in the .38.

Red bloomed a hundred feet above North. In the returning darkness the fire seemed at first like a spotlight through stained glass windows. Then it became ordinary, like a flicker of residual napalm. A common railroad flare cast red light through the broken spirit fences. The Blackbird had set those fireworks as a diversion, in order to light that single flare. The Blackbird was someplace behind the flare. Invisible. The flare put the lower part of the graveyard in silhouette.

North fired. Fired again. The horse emerged from darkness,

and its flank was slick as it limped down the hill.

"Hit him," the Blackbird said. "Hit him, or keep him pinned."

North fired. The muzzle blast was concealed, the explosion muffled. It sounded as if he deliberately fired into the soil of the grave.

Keep him pinned. I aimed. Fired. North screamed. His pistol fired, firing into the grave.

The horse stumbled, and now timid flickers of light began to appear at the edge of the forest. The horse nearly fell into an excavated grave. Blood flowed on the flank, was black in the red light. Too much blood. The horse stumbled directly toward North. In silhouette it seemed as dark and huge as the apocalypse, and it closed on North at an awkward pace—blood, foam. The mouth dripped white.

In red silhouette a white hand and a boot seemed riding directly on the horse's back. The Blackbird was playing Indian tricks. He rode toward North, and he hung on the far side of the horse.

North fired. North began to scream—and I have heard screams, and know them, and know their caliber—and something terrible was happening to North. His pistol sounded as if it had exploded. Soil packed the barrel. Soil plugging the barrel as he fired into the grave.

How many times has this happened, I thought, and scrambled toward North with the pistol pointed—*How many times has the air been full of smoke and cordite and screams—and how much red is there in the world, of fire, of blood; how many times checking the corpses—or shooting them—to be certain they are comfortably dead?*

The horse closed slowly on the screaming North. Blackbird slid to the ground, holding the reins. The eyes of the horse were wide and red in the light of the flare, and the horse carried its wound as it might carry saddlebags filled with lead. It tried to rear, stumbled; the great body nearly falling. It raised a front hoof, white-stockinged, and kicked futilely at North's head. It gasped. Shuddered. It lowered its head, took North's right forearm in its mouth. Lifted. I heard the bone break.

"Let it be," Blackbird said to the horse. He pulled the reins, pulled the horse backward. "Sweet baby let it be."

From the forest, like exhausting waves of surf, points of light shattered across the graveyard. Wind caused whispers as it blew around the reed-like spirit fences.

North was a big man. He took a lot of killing.

He was tenacious as the wind above the forest. He half raised on his left arm, screamed; and his legs moved as he tried to push himself from the plundered grave. I leaned down, trying to turn him over. He was trying to help me. He pushed with his left hand, with his legs—I pulled, trying to turn him and find the wounds—he was stuck in the face of an empty grave. My madness, or his, made it impossible for him to move.

No wound was visible. Only a right arm bent at a wrong angle, a little blood where bone poked through the flesh. Rainwater in the grave was stagnant, smelled putrid, was stained with mud; but not with fresh blood.

In the light of the flare, in the howl of wind, the dancing points of light winked like small arms fire from great distance. The lights were pinpoints of red and white. A red and white surf seemed blown into the graveyard on the voice of a red and white wind.

"How did you know?" I asked the Blackbird. He had shrugged off his jacket, taken off his chambray shirt.

"Gimme your shirt," the Blackbird said. "Forget that thing." He gestured at the screaming North.

I shucked my jacket, my shirt; handed him the shirt.

"Nicked an artery," the Blackbird said. His voice was hollow with grief. "Got to stop it or it'll pump open a big hole."

He tore my shirt into strips. "How did I know?" he grunted. "Kim told me. Of course, Kim coulda been lying." The Blackbird was putting a compress bandage on the horse. "Got to get this fellow to that Indian graveyard before he falls." His voice was low, his black torso visible only beneath flickers of red. "I can't let him die in this place. Man, he was so light and fast. They'd take that away."

In the red light Blackbird's face was a small sculpture of grief. He worked rapidly. "Gonna lose him. I'd give my half-interest in hell for a sewing needle and some catgut." He turned toward North, and North's screams were choking. North's throat must be stripped raw with the screams—and suddenly—and with a rush of fear for my own soul—I realized that I had not really been hearing those screams. They were so common.

"That light show was too real," the Blackbird said. "Maybe this piece of trash"—and he pointed at North—"made it real. Or maybe it really *is* real. That .45 was for us. If North had seen all this before, he knew there wasn't enough bullets in the world."

Blackbird looked at North, at the open mouth which sent scream after scream across the graveyard; routine screams— common and ordinary screams—screams that, in combat, were less interesting than involuntary curses or the wail of the wind over the lip of the jungle.

"I'll make you a deal," the Blackbird said to North. His voice was neutral, neither cruel nor kindly. "You don't deserve it, but I'll make you a deal. You are the man who knows how to laugh. So laugh. If you laugh, I'll pull you out of that hole."

Horror lay somewhere in my mind. It was red, like the flare, as steady as the hand of the wind. It was wide and large back there somewhere, but in the front of my mind was cold pleasure.

North's white face—mud-stained, stained by history—by combat—North's face seemed to flatten as he clenched down on a scream. His face stared from a shallow grave that, for him, was deep as an abandoned quarry. His face concentrated on what it had to do. The left hand brushed at soil on the grave's edge. North's teeth were clenched, then opened. His mouth was a black hollow in the red light. He smiled—lips white and thin and ghastly—a thin-lined and awful smile—chuckled like oily pebbles rattled in a tin can. He forced a laugh, a laugh at history, combat, at us, himself. The sound was thin, nearly weeping.

"Aw man," the Blackbird said, "that ain't no kind of laugh." He gently nudged the horse, the white hand nearly like the guiding hand of a father. The white hand was on the horse's neck, the

143

brown hand held reins to steer the drooping head. Blackbird fumbled for his flashlight. "You got tons of time to practice," he said to North. "Assuming they leave you anything to laugh with."

The small spot of Blackbird's flashlight was like a lightning bug intent on following a line. Blackbird found the trail. His light disappeared downhill. For a short while there was the heavy breathing of the dying horse, the near stumbles; and these were more important than the low, returning screams. North's left hand brushed and clawed on the edge of the grave. Blackbird disappeared toward the Indian graveyard.

I don't know why I stayed behind. Maybe it was the simple combat dictum of 'don't let a dead man kill you': the rule which says that a man who is even a little bit alive can still react. Maybe I stayed because of owing. A man who had saved my life in other days now lay victim of his own betrayal. Worse, I may have stayed because my own death lay somewhere in the future, and I was afraid of those 'mighty old, and powerful' forces the Blackbird had talked about.

"There's all the time there is all the time," the Blackbird had said. Maybe I stayed simply because time was scampering, like the yellow-gloved mouse hands on a watch.

North was a portraiture of red and white. The flare burned and smoked. My flashlight glowed on North's staring eyes. Wind reached for the flare, turned its tip into a tiny furnace. The flare cast crisscrossed shadows as it illuminated the chaos of torn graves and broken spirit fences. North's white face, his white hair, were grotesqueries painted in red light. Breath panted shallow in his mouth. He was no longer able to scream. The broken arm had to be causing enormous pain, but he was engrossed with something greater than pain. The panting face, pale eyebrows knitted in concentration, held not horror; but something worse. The face held the knowledge of horror that was about to arrive.

The wind assumed its proper place and proportion. It began to carry the sounds of distant wails. The wails were thin, and they approached behind the advancing flickers of white. Whiteness lay at the top of the graveyard, as concentrated as a snowstorm. It reached down the hill, obscuring emptied graves, flicking like sparklers from the carved tips of spirit fences. The white seemed like an artist's field, like gessoed canvas on which could be painted the color of screams.

"No man deserves this," I said to North. "Not even you. I would help you if I could."

Perhaps he heard. I would like to believe he heard; that, as his ghastly immortality descended, there was at least one voice which recognized him as having once been human.

The wails rose, and now they were demonic. These were the wails of hunger, wails of the blind; the weeping of hollow faces which had once worn eyes. No gothic cathedral bearing the most awful gargoyles could stand uninvaded by the weeping which now advanced in the tumbling surf of white.

North suffered a last burst of energy. His feet pounded, kicked. He raised on his right elbow, the broken arm askew. He pushed with his left hand. The grave held him firm. The first tongues of whiteness lay at the grave's edge. The wails began to clamor, began to assume hollow and nearly skull-like faces. The first pinpoint of light touched North.

He did not scream. I did. His face was startled. His eyes were wide circles of disbelief, white disks of incredulity. A man sunk in the knowledge of horror, in the knowledge that he would be stripped of everything but hunger; and he was still startled. In the days and months during which the horror had approached—hours of sobriety and hours of drunkenness—no state of mind had prepared him for this.

The points of light were feeding, but not on his body.

I watched, and at first thought the weeping in my soul was for North, for myself, for the Blackbird. North's face went from one shock of startlement to another. As the carpet of white wrapped around him, wailing, wailing, wailing, each shock took him deeper into the horror of loss. No death—by napalm or crucifixion or In- quisition—no death was so terrible as this immortality of hunger.

My weeping increased, from heart to eyes. Sorrow like a field of white filled my mind, body, heart.

Then there was a tug. It was like being nipped by a flea or an ant or an earwig. Fear unlike any I have ever known swelled around me, because the nip was not on the flesh. It was as if a memory had been bitten, some memory of pleasure; sunlight falling through leaves, or shadows and light across the face of a lover. Gone. I backed away. Looked down at North.

So this is how it was with him. His memories of beauty stripped away. The many times his eyes had looked to sea, or looked into rolling banks of Puget Sound mist. Stripped. The calm majesty of the surrounding forest, even the memory of the eternal rain. Stripped.

His face seemed collapsed, already removed from all humanity, yet his mouth still sucked air. His lips were white. Death was due in moments.

There was another tug. Horror was trying to move my legs, trying to make me dash crazily into the red-lined darkness; perhaps to trip and fall into a grave.

Another memory gone. The memory of my daughter as an infant, laughing, creeping across the floor—or the memory of street music tinkling above the heads of crowds in a market.

North's body was dead. The air no longer sucked. The jaw hung loose, and the eyes seemed frozen disks that were fixed staring over the white waves of hell; a white horizon. The slack jaw, the lolling tongue, remained motionless; and deep from what little remained of his spirit, his voice issued. It was a wail. Thin at first. Ascending. Louder. The corpse was wailing North's blindness, his hunger; a pinpoint, a needle of white.

Whiteness was beginning to spread. Flickers danced around me. The wail from North's mouth rose newly toward the sky, searching, hunting, in pursuit.

I fled then. Running, but a cautious run behind the strong beam of the flashlight. Broken fences leaned, open graves were dark mouths. I fled the redness and the whiteness, following the flashlight beam, and plunged into the safety of utter night. Behind me the white points of light ascended above the despoiled graves like the robes of some ancient sorcerer. As I entered the forest trail the graveyard was a concatenation of wails. Spirits were ravishing the already ravished graves.

The Indian graveyard lay as black as the Blackbird's skin. It lay strong as the Blackbird's resolve. On this more level ground trickles of water moved, and wet fir needles gave back pressure of moisture beneath my feet.

I called to the Blackbird as I entered the Indian graveyard. Behind me, in the narrow river of sky above the trail, clouds of whiteness seemed washed here and there by the wind.

The Blackbird did not answer at first. I nearly switched off the flashlight. It made me a target. When Blackbird did answer it was in a subdued voice. I made my way toward him, around the quiet graves enclosed by the oversized beds. The Blackbird sounded sane. I was not; and for moments it seemed that the boiling white clouds behind me were clouds of insanity.

The Blackbird knelt beside the dark shape of the dead horse. Blood pooled on the carpet of fir needles. A large white slug was at the edge of the pool. Blackbird picked it up, looked at it, threw it into the darkness. There was grief in Blackbird's voice, but for me the blood and the dead bulk of the horse were comforts. In the middle of madness at least the bullets had been real.

"Dead," the Blackbird said. I did not know whether he spoke of North or of his horse.

"Finished." My voice sounded the way voices sound after combat. Men ask questions, assure each other that the perimeter is secured.

"Took it pretty hard, did he?"

"It was bad," I said, "worse than he deserved."

"Naw it wasn't," the Blackbird said. "I hope he's trussed like a stuffed pig over a firepit."

"He would have settled for that," I said, "because it was worse than that."

"Well, well," Blackbird said, "that is an elegant thing to hear."

"You weren't there."

"Nope," the Blackbird said, "but I heard the ruckus."

I turned off the flashlight to save the batteries. No cave was ever darker than that forest. In the darkness the serene power of the graveyard was as present as a voice. A question came. Why such unbreachable power here, when up the hill was only despoilation and fury?

"What kind of hell do Indians have?" I was probably speaking to the Blackbird. Maybe to the graveyard.

"Depends on the Indians," the Blackbird said. "Booze, mostly. Little tuberculosis. Bad dreams."

"You know what I mean."

"Mostly they try not to think about it," Blackbird said. "Could be folks build their own. North knocked himself together a real dandy."

The aftermath of combat is always the same. The talk is short. There is no space for tears. What is a man supposed to do? Scream? Screaming doesn't work, because in combat you've already tried it. Sometimes the men scream in their sleep.

"Knew a fellow one time," the Blackbird chuckled—and he did not sound so sane after all—"had to bury his horse. So he dug a hole." The Blackbird was not laughing at his story. Maybe he was laughing at himself, at his memories. "Only after he got the hole dug the horse had stiffened up. Legs stuck out of the hole." The chuckle was not exactly a chuckle, and it was not exactly a sob. I had heard the sound before, but not for many years.

No power in the world could have made me turn on my flashlight. Blackbird was dealing with grief. Blackbird could kill me so quickly that I would not suspect I was being killed.

"So he went to the butcher shop," the Blackbird said, "and he borrowed a meat saw. Cut the legs off. Tossed 'em in the grave. Horse fit just fine."

"I'll help you dig. Help fold the legs before he stiffens."

"I'd be obliged," the Blackbird said. "We'll go get shovels come day. Have to hurry. Whoever finds North is gonna yell 'cop' for forty miles."

I thought of law, of darkness, of history.

Memories of a wet land. Memories of screams. Parachutes. Tan faces. Polished fragments of bone washing from the hills. The Buddha's smile.

I would have to throw the .38 into a river.

We sat in darkness. Men in the business of saving each other's lives. Men who owed; at least that was true if their lives still held enough memories not tinged in fire.

I thought of Miss Molly and hoped her father was well—then I hoped he was dead—then I discovered that I did not like Miss Molly : thoughts disarrayed : all of the nicey-nice people : and I trusted no one but the Blackbird, because the Bird could play the game but he did not order up the game—or purchase it—or applaud it.

"You like being insane," I asked the Bird.

"I don't *like* it," he said, "but I *sure* don't like the other."

"Me too." I giggled. "You've got the sanity of insanity. I've got the law."

"I know a lot about Indians," the Blackbird said, "and *every-thing* about horses."

We folded the horse's legs, and we sat on wet fir needles and leaned our backs against the folded legs to keep them in place as rigor mortis set in. We sat safely in darkness, untouched even by the wind that battered the coast and hills and forest.

For us the darkness was not a curse. We sat waiting for the first touch of morning in the tops of the forest; and sitting, waiting—for the rest of that night, at least—we were safe from the shattering lights of a white and wailing world.

About the Author

Jack Cady has worked as a truck driver, tree high-climber, landscape foreman, auctioneer, and member of the Coast Guard. His writing has attracted an international following; his stories have appeared in *OMNI, Glimmer Train, The Atlantic Monthly, The Yale Review, Svetova Litera-tura, Pulphouse,* in *The Best American Short Stories* (Houghton Mifflin, 1966, 1969, 1970, 1971), and in *Prime Evil* (New American Library, 1988). His books include *The Burning and Other Stories* (University of Iowa Press, 1972) and *The Well* (Arbor House, 1981). He has won the Washington State Governor's Award, the Atlantic "First" Award, the Iowa Prize for Short Fiction, and a recent major fellowship from the National Endowment for the Arts. He currently lives in Washington State, where he teaches at Pacific Lutheran University and writes.

Design by Nick Gregoric.

Text set in Rotation and Gill Sans,
using the KI/Composer and Linotronic 202N.
Typeset by Blue Fescue Typography and Design,
Seattle, Washington.

Broken Moon Press Books are printed on
acid-free, recycled paper exclusively by
Malloy Lithographing, Inc.,
5411 Jackson Road,
Ann Arbor, Michigan 48106.